W. J. Paul

Modern Irish poets by W. J. Paul

W. J. Paul

Modern Irish poets by W. J. Paul

ISBN/EAN: 9783743331044

Manufactured in Europe, USA, Canada, Australia, Japa

Cover: Foto ©Andreas Hilbeck / pixelio.de

Manufactured and distributed by brebook publishing software
(www.brebook.com)

W. J. Paul

Modern Irish poets by W. J. Paul

Modern Irish Poets.

BY

W. J. PAUL.

" Blessings be with them and endless praise
Who gave us nobler loves and nobler cares;
The poets, who on earth have made us heirs
Of truth and pure delight by heavenly lays."
—Wordsworth.

Belfast:
PRINTED BY THE BELFAST STEAM-PRINTING CO., LIMITED,
58, 60, AND 64, ROYAL AVENUE.

1894.

PREFACE.

I N submitting this little volume to the public, I have no apology to make for treading an oft-trodden path. No work of the kind on Irish poets, I believe, has hitherto been published. If apology were needed, it would be because of the limited character of the work, for I have not been able, in the space at my disposal, to include all the living Irish poets. It is my opinion that at no period in the history of Ireland have we had so great poets, and so many of them, as at the present day. I have good grounds for saying that the demand for Irish poetry is on the increase. In corroboration of this fact we have only to reflect on the multitude of volumes recently issued by Irish poets, and *now out of print.* During the last two decades these amount to several hundreds. It is not unnatural, therefore, to expect that readers who have enjoyed so much the works of our native bards and bardesses should wish to know a little about the writers themselves. In these sketches I have endeavoured to place a little information of this kind, in a condensed form, within their reach.

In making the selections, I have not been able in every case to give what I believed to be the best poem of each author. Indeed in many cases the length, or other circumstances, rendered it absolutely impossible for me to do so, but I believe there runs throughout every poem in the book—in a greater or less degree—that undefinable, but no less real, something which is never absent from true poetry.

W. J. PAUL.

Limerick, 1894.

CONTENTS.

—✳✳—

6

PRELUDE.

DEAR Harp of our Country, they wrong thee who say
Thy sweet soul for ever hath vanished away,
That nothing remains of thy glory and power
Any more than of Tara's delightsome sun-bower;
That, broken and mouldered, thy chords can no more
Respond to the touch, as in bright days of yore,
When Carolan conquered all hearts with his song,
And Brian, the Brave, made the winter-night long
To pass like an hour, as, nursed on his knee,
He drew from thy treasures the tones of the free;
Or, Ossian himself swept thy strings to enthral
The chieftains who feasted in lone Cushendall.
Thou art tear-stained, indeed, and black with the grime
Of the years that are gone since the bold Heber's time,
And dark streaks of blood can be seen on thy keys,
Left there by musicians whose sad threnodies
Were wrung out of hearts bleeding sore in their grief
O'er strifes and betrayals of monarch and chief,
And the wrongs and the sorrows of Erin —their own—
From Kerry's grey cashels to fair Innishowen.
But thy Spirit still liveth. We fling back the lie
In teeth of the traitors who whimper and sigh
O'er music departed, and old splendours fled,
O'er mystic charms ended, and tenderness dead ;
Yes! yes! thou art with us, more mellow and sweet
For the long years of danger, with passion replete,
Thou hast seen since the day thou wert happily born
Of the marriage of Art with the mountain-ash lorn ;
And thy power, as ever, melodious and strong,
Bindeth firm to thyself all the lovers of song :
From the bleak, honest North and the warm, sunny South
They gather around thee, true praise in each mouth,
Oh! long may our Country such gratitude see,
And find her true centre of Union in thee.

G. R. B.

Louis H. Victory.

THE literary career of Mr. Louis H. Victory has been a remarkable one. Few writers at his age have added so many and so valuable contributions to

literature. As an essayist, novelist, and poet, he has already made his mark, and those who read his works cannot but be struck with the originality of thought and treatment which characterize his writings.

Mr. Victory was born in Dublin on 15th October, 1870. From a very early age his taste for literature began to manifest itself. At the age of twelve his favourite enjoyment was to get into a secluded place with a copy of Shakespeare's works; and so persistently, at this period, did he pore over an old copy, in which the print was very small, that he nearly lost his eyesight before the cause was found out. To have such a congenial companion occupying so little space was to him a great source of enjoyment. At that tender age he could repeat most of the text of "Hamlet"—a character which, he avers, has influenced him more than any other, in or out of fiction. Shakespeare is, beyond all others, his favourite author, and indeed his admiration for the works of this great writer is unbounded. At the age of seventeen Mr. Victory received an appointment on the staff of a Dublin newspaper, where for the next three years he was employed in reporting lectures, notable sermons, &c., which at that age he was able to do *verbatim*. Since then he has written over two score of short stories, most of which have been published in the Dublin newspapers, and a number of novels. The most notable of his prose works of fiction is a romance entitled "Lady Rosalind," published by Messrs. Digby, Long & Co., London. When first issued it was extensively criticised by the London and Provincial Press, and there seemed to be a general consensus of opinion among the critics that the gifted author had produced a work of exceptional merit. He has written a great many essays, the most important of which is a series of "Studies in Shakespeare's Plays," for which his early reading eminently fitted him, and which he himself believes is his worthiest contribution to literature. We think, however, that his poetry has attracted more attention than anything else he has produced. He commenced to publish his poems in the year 1891, and his first, which was a Shakespearian sonnet entitled " A Faithful Dog," was published in the *Weekly Irish Times* of that year. He has since contributed over one hundred poems, chiefly sonnets (Shakespearian and Italian forms) and lyrics, to the columns of the same paper. In 1893 he issued a volume of his poetical works under the modest title of " Collected Verses." This work contains many choice flowers of thought, and throughout the book there is an entire absence of monotony, repetition of ideas, and sameness of expression.

If the past forms any index to the future, we are led to anticipate a brilliant career for this talented young author.

THE SOUL OF JUDAS.

A DREAM OF PUNISHMENT.

WHEN Judas died, his sin-empurpled soul
Sped—quickly as a God-thought speeds to earth —
On high into the ether 'tween the stars,
And fluttered towards the transcendental gates
That in their blinding brilliancy, enfold
From view of all things unbeatified
The sempiternal glories of high Heaven!
The soul of Judas, guilty with Christ's blood,
Sought entrance thro' those sun-bright gates of Heaven ;
But from the dazzling brightness flashed a soul—
An angel-soul of wondrous loveliness—
And hurled the God-man's murderer back from Heaven
To wander—like an outcast from the realms

Of God and man—throughout the dim abyss
Of interstellar space. Then fled it down
The trackless ether where no waves of light
E'er cross the Stygian gloom, unsearchable.
But there no rest the soul of Judas found!
Then hied it, in a hopeless agony,
Unto the fœtid entrance gates of hell,
And craved admittance there. But, lo! at once
A phalanx of discordant sounds arose
From out the seething sulphur of dark hell:
A million million damnéd souls cried out—
"Avaunt! thou murderer of the Son of God!"
And then a million million devils came
All hissing—"Hence, you scarlet-tainted shape!
By crucifying Jesus you withheld
From us some myriad souls that else were ours!
Begone! not e'en such rest as hell affords
Shall ever now be yours!" And speaking thus,
The devils drove the soul of Judas far
In dim remoteness from their black abyss.
Writhing in agony, beyond all pains
Of earth or hell, the wandering soul pursued
Its unrewarded, nay, accurséd search
For some soul-habitation where to dwell.
It fled from star to star, from sphere to sphere,
But everywhere it was denied a home,
Till weary of its interstellar flight,
It fell, pain-fluttering, to the earth again.
It wandered, like some ghost, into a wood,
Amid whose sombrous boughs the trancing notes
Of one lone nightingale made musical
The erstwhile pulseless peace that reignéd there.
"Ah! let me dwell enfeathered in your form!"
The soul of Judas craved in language known,
But inarticulate. And straight the bird,
Affrighted, ceased to sing, and winged its flight
To some unknown retreat. The wandering soul

Then sought a snail that crawled along the ground;
" You meanest thing that grovels on this earth,
Will *you* afford a dwelling for this soul
That vainly seeks for any kind of home ?"
The lowly snail shrank far within its shell,
In mute denial of the outcast's quest.
And now from out the darkness of the wood
The astral form appeared of Him who died
In torture on the Cross of Calvary !
The soul of Judas shuddered at the sight.
" I pray, Thee, God, in mercy's sacred name,
Send me to blackest hell or to some place
More horrible than hell.   But do not come   .
With those sad eyes of Thine, with bleeding hands
And side and feet, and with that crown-pierced head,
To torture me.   All other agony
I'll bear unmurmuring, but save me *this* !"
So pleaded Judas in the forest depths ;
But, since that moment, now long decades gone,
The soul of Judas wanders peacelessly
Throughout the baseless realms of boundless space.
All vainly seeking to evade the Christ
Whose blood-stained astral haunts him evermore !
From star to star, from sphere to sphere it hies,
But everywhere it sees the haunting form
Of Jesus crucified !   It vainly asks
For mercy.   When its piteous wail is heard
The spheres yield back one answer—*only one*—
" This is the punishment of that red soul
That crucified the Son of the Most High !"

THE LILY.

Night brooded over lone Gethsemane ;
And 'neath the shade of one tall sobbing tree
The Son of God knelt down, and wept, and prayed ;
He writhed and groaned beneath the burden laid
Upon His spirit by the sins of men

Until His soul was over-wrought and then
Great beads of blood burst from His sacred brow.
He cried "My Father if it may be now
O, take away this bitter load from me!
But if, by Thy wise will, this may not be—
If this dread chalice may not pass away—
Great God, Thy will be done, I humbly pray!"
Then Jesus staggered weakly to His feet
And, doing so, He heard the woods repeat
The words that He had sent on high to God,
When His rent form lay stretched upon the sod.
But lo! while yet His heart was torn with sighs,
A touching vision swam before His eyes:
He saw through all the terrors of His grief,
That every blade of grass and every leaf
Bent down and wept great glistening pearly tears,
While God's hot wrath was ringing through the spheres!
Then every flower, save one, bent down its head—
The snow-white Lily stayed erect and said—
" Great God, Thou knowest that I am white and pure;
Why, then, should I humility endure ?"
Then calmly to the stately flower Christ turned —
While in His heart the fire of love fast burnéd ;—
And in unangered tones He softly said,
With lips now stained unnaturally red—
" The purest thing that in the world could be
Might well be sad, and weep at sight of me.'
The Lily, by these words, of pride bereft,
Bowed humbly down and sorrowfully wept.

THE POET.

"Vex not thou the poet's mind
For thou can'st not fathom it."

AH list! what is that weird, enchanting strain
That floats to me, allaying Nature's pain ?
What is that soul-entrancing harmony
That brings before me vistas heavenly ?

You laugh and lightly say, no strain you hear!
But, there it is again, and yet more clear!
Ah me! I had forgot, you lack the ear
That hears the music of the heavenly sphere;
You say the sound is false, that I am mad!
Well, if to hear transcendent sounds divine,
To catch Empyrean visions' winged outline,—
If *this* be. madness, I am gladly mad!
Remember, that the poet knows a joy
That soulless scoffers never can destroy.

TO THE ROBIN.

SWEET robin redbreast, while I hand thee bread
I marvel why thy silky breast is red;
And then I ask myself can it be true,
The story that I heard of Christ and you!
For it is said that while to Calvary
The Saviour bore the Crucifixion tree
A robin paused upon His sacred head
And picked a thorn from out His crown, stained red,
When, lo! the blood that oozed forth—blood most blest,
Dropped down and stained the robin's stainless breast,
And ever since that fateful, hallowed day
Thy breast, sweet bird, is red, the legends say!
Thrice blessèd bird, thrice welcome to my bread,
Since on thy breast is blood from Jesus' head.

Michael Hogan,

BARD OF THOMOND.

⸺◆◆⸺

MR. MICHAEL HOGAN, " Bard of Thomond," was born at Thomondgate, Limerick, on the 31st October, 1828. His father was a wheelwright, and a real handy man he was. He was also an excellent musician. He could play the flute and the violin; and the instruments on which he played were the workmanship of his own hands. When a child, young Michael used to enjoy immensely the evenings when his father played for the amusement of the family and neighbours who frequented his friendly hearth, to listen to the fine old Irish airs discoursed so tenderly on the violin, many of which, the Bard declares, have not been heard of since the death of his father.

In the early part of his career Mr. Hogan received no school education. He was, what he now terms, "a wild youth," and when sent to school he immediately set about lampooning the scholars, and even the teachers, and was instantly turned home. He was not long, however, of learning to read and write. He would get a lead pencil and paper and copy the headings of books, or a word of large print from the advertising columns of a newspaper without knowing what the words were— merely imitating the copy. By being told the words, and the letters composing them, in a short time he learned to read and *print*—not write. This practice of printing he continued, and ever afterwards he could print faster than he could write.

Mr. Hogan's first published poems appeared in the *Celt*. He afterwards wrote for the "Irishman," "Nation," "Munster News," and recently for the "Limerick Leader." In 1851 he collected a little volume of his works, entitled "Lays and Legends of Thomond," which was published in Dublin, and in 1867 a larger collection under the same title. This volume created a favourable impression on the minds of the public, and established the Bard's claim to recognition and public favour as a true born son of song. It was enthusiastically received, and was quickly bought up.

The career of the poet was pretty smooth, and devoid of much public interest until he commenced the publication of a series of satires. These made him become the object of admiration to some, to others the object of fear or execration. He had a thorough command of cutting language, and when the prominent public men got out of his graces, as they so often did, he came down on them with merciless severity. Their lack of appreciation of him preyed so much on his mind that he determined to "give the citizens a bit of his mind concerning these great men." In 1869 he commenced a series of publications entitled SHAWN-A-SCOOB (John-a-broom). These satirical pamphlets—eight in number, issued at various periods—were directed against the Mayor, Corporation, and other public men, impeaching them with "high crimes and misdemeanours." The public interest in their issue was great. Their circulation was enormous, and the sensation produced by them was something unprecedented during the past half century. An outline of the general nature of them may be gleaned from the following stanza which occurs at the beginning of the eighth number. It is entitled "The Bard's Pastoral," and is dedicated to "All who don't like it" :—

> "The world's a hive of vagabonds,
>   The Church a nest of knaves,
>   The State a den of scoundrels,
>   And the land a mart of slaves.
>   Princes, prelates, dukes and lords,
>   Are found a common clan,
>   But 'tis the Devil's job on earth
>   To find an honest man."

During the Parliamentary elections of 1880 he published another satire, on the title-page of which was "The Pictorial Gallery of the Limerick Election.   A graphic illustration of the conspicuous characters and talents of the sublime orators who so magnificently figured on that most memorable occasion, by the Bard of Thomond."   The contents may be fairly guessed by the title.   About the same time he published a companion volume to this one.   It was entitled "O'Shaughnessy's Dodging and Gabbett's Tomfoolery."   Messrs. O'Shaughnessy and Gabbett were the Parliamentary candidates, and to neither of them did the Bard offer one word of praise.   In 1883 he published "Cupid's Adventure," which was the last of his satirical productions.   Without commenting on the wisdom of the Bard's action in publishing these pamphlets (which, if they brought him pecuniary advantage, made him many enemies), it is not too much to say that they exhibit rare powers for versification and the power of expressing thought in terse and vigorous language.   These satires have never been republished, and are long since out of print.   They are not included in the general collection of his "Lays and Legends of Thomond."   This portly volume, the latest edition of which was published in 1880 by Messrs. Gill & Son, Dublin, contains a mine of interesting poetry, ballads of war and chivalry brimful of martial fury, legends full of enchantment and fairy music, humorous songs thoroughly Irish in sentiment and full of the richest melody.

Mr. Hogan lived for some years in a beautiful little cottage which he built for himself on the right bank of the Shannon. Here he reclaimed a piece of waste land from the river to enlarge his garden, and built a summer-house in which he penned his famous dramatic ballad, "The Bard and the Shannon." Through a series of reverses, however, he was obliged to part with it, and when leaving it he wrote another pathetic ballad entitled "Farewell to the Shannon." For some time afterwards he was without any fixed occupation or income. In the year 1886 he went to America, where he remained for three years. He wrote some short poems after his return home, but it was not long until his eyesight gave up, and so deficient has it become of late that he has practically "ceased his warblings." He is now in the employment of the City Corporation, his duties being merely nominal. All former unpleasantnesses have been forgotten, and the genial Bard is the pride not only of the Corporation but of the citizens generally.

THE BANSHEE AND THE GREAT EARL OF THOMOND.

FROM the clouds of the hill, and the gloom of the night,
Who is she that appears like the wintry-moon, white ?
The cold dew is gleaming, like beads, on her hair,
And she rings her gaunt hands, with a shriek of despair !

Look, Earl! the Spectre stands full in thy path,
And her angry face beareth a mission of wrath;
There's a mist round her form that's awful to see,
And her eyes, like blue wild-fire, are turned upon thee!

The Earl rein'd in his black war-horse, and gazed,
With his sword turned down, and his visor upraised;
And he saw standing out on a cliff, in his way,
The dismal, White Woman of lonely Craiglea.
One hand she outstretched, like a skeleton bough,
And one was close-press'd to her cold stony brow;
While her lips breathed curses that awfully fell,
On his spirit and brain, like the sentence of hell.

"The mighty of Erin is laid on the earth,
And her war-lions, bleeding, have fled to the North;
For thou, curst apostate! hast reddened thy steel
With the glorious heart's blood of the clans of O'Neill!
May the rank steam of death from that red slaughter field
Where you taught the proud Chieftains of Ulster to yield,
Be shaped to a scourge by the finger Divine,
To wound, waste and wither the slaves of thy line!

"O Chiefs of Kincora! immortal in song!
Whose arms flashed death 'mid the fierce battle throng,
With scorn, look down from your high dwelling-place,
On the slave-making recreant who sprang from your race!
In their grandeur and might, did those chiefs ever dream
That their offspring would cover their glory with shame?
Did they from their shores the grim sea-robbers chase,
For their sons to be servants to robbers more base?
        .   .   .   .

"Perdition will grasp the low heirs of thy line,
And the death-curse of freedom brand all that is thine!
Till its vengeance shall leave not a stone of thy walls,
Nor a fire on thy hearth, nor a slave in thy halls!
Eternal contempt on the day you went forth,
With the Saxon to crush the Red Hand of the North!

Hark ! the cry of your country rings up from her tomb ;
' Assassin of Erin ! Lord Thomond, go home !'

" Go home, you apostate ! and drink your red wine !
May the odour of corpses be round where you dine !
And the tears of gaunt widows mix black in your bowl,
And the cry of starved orphans strike hard at your soul !
Go home—may the charnel pits, gory and deep—
Where your countrymen fester—bring balm to your sleep !
May your soul feast on visions of famine and flames,
And the death-shriek of Erin be heard in your dreams !"

PADDY MacCARTHY TO HIS BRIDGET MacSHEEHY.

ARRAH, Bridget MacSheehy, your eyes are the death o' me,
And your laugh, like a fairy sthroke, knocks out the breath o' me !
The devil a cobweb of slumber, till dawn'd the day,
Has cum to my lids, while the long night I yawn'd away !
Och, you heart-killing imp, 'twas your witchery puzzled me,
Like a bird by a night-wisp, your beauty has dazzled me !
I'd rather be forty miles running away wid you,
Than live to be parted, ten minutes, one day wid you ! ·

'Pon my soul, I was dhraming last night that you came to me
Wid your own purty smile, like a sweet drink of cream to me,
Says you, " Paddy Carthy, I'm coming to marry you !"
" Och, my jewel," says I, " to his Riverince I'll carry you !"
So I thought my poor heart gave a thump, like a prize-fighter,
As off to the chapel I jump'd, like a lamplighter ;
But scarce had the priest time to see how his robe was on,
When—och, blood an' turf !—I awoke ere the job was done !

Now troth 'tis a heartache, betune you an' I, Biddy !
To let that sly rogue of a dhrame tell a lie, Biddy !
If your sweet mouth just says, " My dear boy, here's my hand to
    you !"
By the lord of Kilsmack ! Paddy Carthy will stand to you !

In the meadow I'll mow, in the haggard I'll work for you;
Say the word, an' I'll walk on my head to New York for you
My heart wid the heat of devotion so beats for you,
'Tis just like a little child crying for sweets to you !

There's Judy Moloney, wid ten on the watch for her—
Her uncle cum to me to make up a match for her ;
There's Thady Mulready, by Loch Quinlan's water, clear,
Faith, he'd gi' me six cows if I'd marry his daughter, dear !
But no, by the powers ! I wud rather go beg wid you,
Hopping from village to town on wan leg wid you,
Than be walking on two, wid a rich heiress stuck to me;
If I'm not speaking true to you, darling, bad luck to me !

You're the queen of the lilies that grow up so tenderly ;
An' your leg is as fair as white wax, moulded slenderly
The berries are so like your lips that the pick of 'em,
I pluck'd from the bush till I ate myself sick of 'em !
Where the hawtree its flowers to the sunbeams is handing up
I saw, like your white neck, a blossom-branch standing up,
I climb'd to get at it—you'd pity the trim o' me—
For, bad luck to the thorns, they carved every limb o' me !

I'll purchase the best wedding ring in the town for you !
Or, by thunder, to make one, I'd pull the moon down for you;
If I cud lay my hand on the sun for a crown for you,
Sure I'd be the boy wud win light and renown for you !
Now, Biddy, my jewel ! what have you to say to me ?
Just give up your heart without farther delay to me ;
And I will bless this as a glorious fine day to me—
If a queen got such courting, by Jove, she'd give way to me !

THE BATTLE OF CROOM.
A.D. 1599.

LORD ESSEX is coming—and deep is the gloom
Of his banners o'er shading the borders of Croom—
Up—up ye fierce men of the mountain and glen,
And raise your loud warshouts of freedom again !

Like the dark mists of winter o'erspreading the vale
The plumes of the Saxon float proud on the gale :
Like the waves of the river, when lit by the sun,
The steel-sheathed ranks in their splendour move on.

The war-fires are lighted—oh! princely MacCaura!
Haste—sharpen thy sword for the combat to-morrow!
Let thy proud banner wave o'er the battles red brow,
And hurl thy clan on the ranks of the foe!

Arise to the contest, ye brave Geraldines!
Array the fierce war-horse, and marshall your lines!
Come forth to the field, like the dash of the sea,
When the temptest-cloud bursts upon stormy Kilkee!

The red sun is bright on the hills of Clan Carrha—
They sweep to the fight, like the death-winged arrow ;
The wild battle slogan, tremendous and stern,
Swells fierce, on the wind, from the ranks of the kern.

The blaze and the clash of the combat began,
And God's burning terror seem'd wielded by man ;
From the Gael to the Saxon one flame-deluge burned,
And fiercely the Saxon his vengeance returned.

As the mountain-cloud, chafed by the wind-spirit's ire,
Spits the red-winged flash from its black mouth of fire ;
So furious and fast did Clan Carrha's fierce sons,
On the proud Saxon host pour the blaze of their guns.

The mail'd phalanx bursts where the wild Gallowglass,
With his ponderous axe, thro' the ranks hewed a pass ;
While the armour that guarded their hearts' purple wells,
Rang lond, as the clashing of iron-tongued bells.

Have you heard, at deep midnight, the sea-surges rave,
When the tempest king dances in fire on the wave ?
So dire was the fury of axes and spears,
As they plough'd the strong mail of the tall cavaliers.

Like reeds on the river-bank, trampled and strown,
Lie footmen and horsemen together o'erthrown ;
Hark ! the wild cheer of victory—Lord Essex has fled,
And the flower of his legions behind him lies dead.

There's triumph and joy in the homes of the Gael,
There's wailing and woe in the towers of the Pale ;
The Saxon is swept from the plains of Clan Carrha,
And Desmond is free as her wild Gougane Barra.

Reb. G. R. Buick, M.A.

THE Rev. George Raphael Buick, M.A., author of
numerous poems scattered over the pages of magazines
and newspapers, is a clergyman of the Irish Presbyterian
Church.   He was educated at the Royal Academical
Institution, Belfast, and afterwards at the Queen's College
in the same city.   His career while attending the latter,
which he entered in 1858, was a brilliant one.   During
each of the three years of his undergraduate course he
held a junior scholarship in mathematics, won numerous
prizes in several other departments, such as Natural
History, Geology and Chemistry, and closed his course of
attendance by gaining the Senior Scholarship in Chemistry.
In 1861 he graduated as Bachelor of Arts of the Queen's
University, obtaining First Honours and the Gold Medal
in Experimental Sciences.   In 1862 he repeated the
performance, carrying off First Honours, and the Gold
Medal again at the examination for Master of Arts degree.
He subsequently entered the Presbyterian College, Belfast,
where he also distinguished himself : among other things,
for any essay on " The Influence of the Crusades on

Commerce." Having finished his collegiate training he was ordained to the ministry of the Presbyterian Church in February, 1868, at Cullybackey, in the County of Antrim, where he has continued to reside ever since.

Mr Buick is an ardent antiquarian, and has done good service in investigating the pre-historic remains of his native county. Several important papers of his will be found in "The Journal of the Royal Historical and Archælogical Association of Ireland," in the "Proceedings of the Society of Antiquaries of Scotland," and in "The Journal of the Royal Society of Antiquaries, Ireland." He is a member of the Royal Irish Academy, and is one of the Vice-Presidents of the Royal Society of Antiquaries. He is widely read on a great variety of subjects, and his extensive Library, as well as his Collection of Antiquities is known to every lover of science and literature for many miles around. He is intimately acquainted with most of the leading *litterateurs* and scientists in the North of Ireland, with whom his opinions have great weight. His unassuming manner, his kindly nature and genial disposition make him a pleasing companion and welcome visitor. His first published poems appeared in Cassell's publications in 1866. Since then he has been a regular contributor to current literature. He has keen powers of observation, refined taste, and the art of melodious expression. His descriptions of local scenery are singularly fresh and accurate. Long may he continue to enrich Irish literature with his contributions, and find enjoyment in describing the beautiful scenery of his native place " beside the Maine."

IN PRAISE OF SLEMISH.

SERENE and strong old Slemish stands,
  A goodly sight to see,
Upspringing from the winsome lands,
  Where Braid's white homesteads be.

In rugged grandeur, glorified
  With mellowing mist and haze,
He smiles across the valley wide
  Where Maine her course delays;

Or looks far off to catch the gleam
  Of sapphire tinted wave
By Garron's cliffs, or by the stream
  Near Ossian's lonely grave.

A sturdy peak—he forceful lifts,
  Above the long hill range,
His head sublime to where the rifts
  Of cloudland glow and change,

As one, who filled with calm content
  In Christ, and clear of fraud,
And confident through pure intent,
  Lifts up the face to God.

Ringed round with belt of moorland lone,
  And flanked with fertile fields,
Right well he figures forth in stone
  The men our Ulster yields.

A rugged race, if manners make
  The chief, or only, rule;
But staunch, and true, and strong to take
  High place in camp and school.

Ah! how that mountain rising sheer
  Our Antrim hills among,
Has moved my heart from year to year,
  And round me glamour flung;

And drawn my soul from out itself
    To wisdom, love, and truth ;
And helped me fight 'gainst hate and pelf,
    And sins that stain hot youth ;

And made the lines, all stark and stiff,
    Of life and simple duty
To curve and flow with grace, as if
    They nothing knew but beauty.

So was it when a happy youth
    I sat at Nature's knee,
And sought to learn her hidden truth
    And grasp her alchemy ;

So was it when in manhood's ways
    I found " the Dead Sea fruit,"
And hatred reaped instead of praise,
    And almost failed to boot ;

And now I'm old and out of touch
    With men and things of might,
He brings me strength, and peace, and much
    Of winterless delight ;

For gazing out from that fair slope
    Where I have toiled till now,
I see him calm, and strong in hope,
    The sunshine round his brow.

As though no storm had stirred for long
    His heath-plumed oriflamme,
And I am strong as he is strong,
    And calm with finer calm.

O dear old hill ! What memories sweet,
    Like crystals round a thread,
Grow sharp and clear, and gather fleet
    About thy storied head !

Could'st thou but gain the gift of speech,
   Or play the part of bard,
What startling sermons thou wouldst preach,
   What songs thy friends reward.

The mammoth played about thy base
   When first thou rose in air,
Huge deer, with horns three yards apace,
   Beside thee made their lair.

And later far, the Firbolgs came,
   And Tuath-de-Danaan,
To spill each other's blood, and claim
   The soil of Partholan.

In vain—the race of Heremon
   Swept in to grasp the prize,
And soon from Boyne to Cruachan
   Queen Scota's banner flies.

The years go by; alas! with blood,
   For Usna's sons betrayed,
The North is red—the crimson flood
   Leaps up to lap thy shade.

And later still, the Red Branch Knights,
   From Navan of the Forts,
Made land-mark of thy rounded heights
   When bound for Northern ports.

And many a hostile band from Mourne,
   And many a fierce Ard-Ree,
On mail-clad chargers gaily borne,
   Rode past saluting thee.

All bent on fame and bloody fray,
   Or tribute sworn to take
From false-tongued monarchs far away,
   Or dwellers of the lake.

For those were days when might was right,
  And safety stood in steel,
And clansmen found the joys of fight
  With Cormac or O'Neill.

But what of these! they sink and pale,
  As near the sun the star,
In light of that transcendent tale—
  The Christ's own Holy War.

That story—like to robe inwrought
  With gems and braided dyes—
All richly dight with true-love knot
  And thread of sacrifice.

Wherein is told, how Milchu's slave,
  Young Patrick, far from home
Sought Him whose hand alone can save
  On Skerry's whin-clad dome;

Or, at thine own broad altar stone,
  High lifted up in air,
Made oft to heaven his humble moan
  And learnt the power of prayer.

And how when free and home returned,
  He thought on Erin dear,
Till love took shape and hotly burned
  To preach the Gospel here.

He came, he taught the Blessed Word :
  The living message sped—
Our island bowed to Christ the Lord—
  The Druid faith fell dead.

Now glory to our Triune God,
  Whose own the islands be,
That this green land of ours was trod
  By saint so sage as he;

That one in heart, so Christly hale,
   Gave life and love to light
Those holy flames foredoomed to pale
   The fires of Pagan night.

O Slemish! stand the centuries through
   As thou hast stood till now,
His hallowed haunts to guard anew, —
   His fame about thy brow!

And when our Antrim men and maids
   Look up from hill and heugh
To mark thy soft and sheeny shades,
   Thy well beloved blue,

Oh! may their hearts rise higher still,
   In sweet and glad accord,
From Patrick's memory haunted hill
   To Patrick's Triune Lord.

BESIDE THE SEA.

IN a green and golden valley,
   Close beside the sapphire sea,
Where the streamlets love to dally
   And the breezes blow so free,
Dwells a happy little maiden
   Full of merriment and glee,
Yet withal, her heart is laden,
   Laden deep with love for me.

Maiden fairer saw you never,
   And she's good and true as fair,
Art and fashion do not sever
   Love and truth from beauty there.
And I know she loves me ever,
   That her heart of hearts I share
By the way her lips will quiver
   And her half caressant air.

And I love her, oh! I love her,
    With a love as pure and true,
Though they say I rank above her
    And a higher mate should woo.
Yes, I love her for her beauty;
    And for more than beauty, too,
For her simple sense of duty,
    And her faith so fresh and new.

Yonder, where the western beaches
    Smile in all their silver pride;
Where each mountain shadow reaches
    Down to kiss the lust'rous tide,
Often meet we two at even,
    Often wander side by side
And, somehow, I'm nearer heaven
    There than in the world outside.

God ever bless thee, dearest maid,
    For the love thou hast for me;
And may His blessing soon be said
    On our union that's to be;
And may He grant me health and strength
    To smooth the path of life for thee,
When, for my sake, thou'st left at length
    Thy pleasant home beside the sea.

BESIDE THE MAINE.
(A CULLYBACKEY SONG).

OH! green and gay the beeches be
    Which grow beside the Maine;
And sweet the bloom of hawthorn tree
    When May is on the wane.

The blue that lights the laughing eyes
    Of speed-well through the Dreen,
Might well provoke the longing sighs
    Of Beauty's peerless Queen.

And never yet was music made
   From harp, or reed, or lute,
Might match the merry strathspeys played
   Where Low Park shallows shoot.

But what to me is bloom, or tree —
   The floweret's cobalt gleam
Or yet the merriest symphony
   Beat out by gladsome stream !

They weary me ! They dreary be !
   They fill my heart with pain !
My love is dead ! God pity me !
   She sleeps beside the Maine.

OUT OF THE DEPTHS.

" Restore unto me the joy of Salvation."—Ps. 51.

OUT of the darkness, and out of the deep,
   Where the waves of sorrow around me sweep,
And the lurid flashes of lightning leap
   From crest to curve of each billowy steep,
Ah ! what can I do but cry unto Thee,
   My God ! O my God ! have mercy on me.

My bark it is frail, it should not be here,
   Where the winds are wild and the rocks so near,
But my heart was wilful, and self would steer,
   Regardless of chart, or of check, or fear,
And now the danger is dreadful to see !
   My God ! O my God ! have mercy on me.

I have sinned, I have sinned, I wrongly thought
   That afar from Thee, and by Thee forgot,
I might safely sail, nor look out for aught
   Save for seas all calm and with spoils all fraught,
I discard such hopes—I make this my plea—
   O my God ! my God ! have mercy on me.

I sink, I am lost, my sad fears increase,
  Speak, Saviour, speak, bid the fierce storm cease;
Come over the billows, and then in the peace
My bark shall be safe, my sorrows surcease,
I'll know Thee, and love Thee, and bow down the knee,
  When thus, O my God, Thou hast mercy on me.

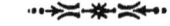

Kathleen Knox.

MISS KATHLEEN KNOX is daughter of the late Charles George Knox, Esq., LL.D., for many years Vicar-General of Down and Connor, and the younger brother of the late Lord Primate, Dr. Knox.

Miss Knox commenced her literary career when a mere school-girl, and her first efforts which appeared in print were published in the *Belfast Weekly Whig* when she was little more than a child. When she came to maturer years she forsook poesy for a time, and wrote several books, fairy tales, and other little stories for children. Some of these were published in London by Messrs. Griffith & Farran, and some in Belfast by Messrs. Marcus Ward & Co. Later on she wrote a three volume novel which was published by Smith, Elder & Co., and was favourably received by the public. In 1888 she returned to poetry, and issued a little work called "The Islanders" under the *nom de plume* of "Edward Kane," which, though it showed much vigour of thought and originality of conception, and was highly commended by several eminent critics, did not meet with a reception so general nor so enthusiastic as her previous publications. During the last few years Miss Knox has written a considerable

number of short poems. These have been mostly published
in the local newspapers ; and at the competition for prizes
offered by the *Belfast Weekly News* she has often been
successful in obtaining the first prize. The following are
all prize poems, and recently obtained :—

DREAMS.

OH that the night would meet the night,
And never the world be sad with light ;
Light is for pleasure, and gold and glee—
      Darkness for me !

Oh that the day, the garish day,
With its golden glory would pass away.
Sweet is the sun, but the gentle night
      Hath a sweeter light :

A light that o'er all the earth is spann'd,
The light that was " never on sea or land,"
The light from a long-lost world, that streams
      The light of dreams.

Dear darkness, come, look on me again
With the eyes that I never have sought in vain,
Bring back that world, which I used to know
      In the long ago !

Oh, come with that darkness to me sweet night,
To those who have loved not, be given the light,
To those who have lost not, the garish beams —
      For me, my dreams !

LONELINESS.

OVER the level lawn
My love, my maiden, I watched, and I thrilled as I saw her pass,
      Fair as the silver dawn,
Daintily pressing the dew, from the tender blades of the grass.
      Into the wildwood glen.

Where the roses first awake, and the lilies blow by the stream,
  My maiden came, and then
We whispered a word and went—or was it only a dream ?
  Up to the sunset glow,
Right over the hills all day, we wandered hand in hand,
  And I spoke to her, soft and low,
While the sunset glory died, and the shadows lay over the land.
  She heard me and smiled and wept,
Wept in her joy, dear heart, that her love was a thing to say :—
  Oh, surely my heart hath slept,
Or was it a year ago ? nay twenty years to-day.
  And the sun behind the hill
Hath never risen again, and bare is the wildwood glen,
  And the world is living still,
But I am alone and dead, and never have lived since then.

NIGHT.

A SONNET.

WE live between two worlds, the Day and Night!
One is the garment of our common thought,
The space wherein a little work is wrought
And much, that has no fellowship with light.
The other—a soft darkness is its might,
With stars and dreams its gentleness is fraught ;
Some deep and quiet lessons it has taught,
And prayer has built an altar in its sight.

Shall we not love thee, then, benignant Power!
Whether on mountain heights thou broodest dim,
Or layest a short spell on city ways.
Whether thou scatter far thy dewy dower
Of happy sleep, or linger long with him
Whose deep heart for his fellows, wakes and prays.

A SPRING EVENING.

TENDER and still, with the rush of rain
On the fresh young saplings, now and again,
Are the secret places, where seems to float
The rich sad thrill of the thrush's note.

'Tis not the nightingale's song of woe,
The love and the sorrow of long ago!
The thrush's song is the yearning strain
Of the hope that comes with storm and rain.

Oh sad spring even! It seems to say,
Hope, still hope, for the summer day!
Oh wayward spring, with her smiles and tears!
Hope, still hope, for the hope of years!

Hope, still hope! And my heart has heard
The sweet spring song of the thicket bird;
And my heart takes heart, and hopes again,
That the clouds return not, after the rain!

Alessie Faussett.

THIS popular and highly gifted poetess was born on
8th January, 1841. Her father, Rev. William Bond·
was Rector of Ballee Parish Church, Co Down. Early
in life she began to compose verse, and her genius and
ability as a poetess quickly gained public acknowledgment. She is represented by one or more contributions
in several eminent collections, including "The Church
Hymnal," "Lyra Hibernica Sacra," some of Cassell's publications, and "Wanklyn's Church of England Lectionary
illustrated by Poets." Among other publications she is the
author of the following volumes:—"Thoughts on Holy

Words," 1867. " Triumph of Faith, and other Poems,"
1870. " The Cairns of Iona," 1873 " Rung In, and
other Poems," 1880, and " From Quiet Ways," 1882.

In 1875 she was married to the Rev. Henry Faussett,
Rector of Edenderry, near Omagh, Co. Tyrone.

Mrs. Faussett holds a high place among the hymn
writers of the present generation, and her name and
writings are as familiar in literary circles in Great Britain
as they are at home. Her poems are chiefly on religious
subjects, and the high ideal she has of the importance of
Scriptural teaching is plainly evident. They are distinguished by a fervent tone of deep religious feeling,
and there is a melodiousness about them which at once
proclaims the true poet. Their beauty of thought, elegance
of diction, and sweetness of expression make them enjoy-
able as well as profitable reading.

THE SHUTTING OF THE GATES OF DERRY.

IT was the time of Advent,
Two hundred years ago,
Or years well-nigh two hundred,
When the clouds hung dark and low ;
When o'er the Foyle was danger,
And crime from near and far
Came rushing on our city,
Like springtide on the bar :

'Twas then amid the darkness
The light of faith was seen,
And grandly to their duty
Sprang forth the brave Thirteen.*

---

* It is believed to be from the phrase in this poem that the " Apprentice
Boys " have been locally, and then generally, called " The Brave Thirteen."

'Tis Truth they hold, to die for!
  'Tis ruin that awaits
One moment's indecision—
  But they have shut the gates.

It was the time of Advent,
  Isaiah's words were read—
(Not less to us for ever
  Than to our sainted dead!)
The Psalms of faith and valour—
  The glorious Acts of old—
For all the Church's warfare
  And long endurance told.

No marvel, then, they nerved them
  To stem oppression's flood!
No marvel that our fathers
  Resisted unto blood!
That mention of surrender,
  Indignant, they struck dumb,
And harder far than battle,
  Endured till help should come.

They kept their iron Christmas,
  They spent their stormy spring,
Within their walls embattled,
  Their old enchanted ring.
'Mid crashing bombs they lifted
  On high the dauntless head,
And vow'd more deep devotion
  Beside their martyr'd dead.

Still on our darkness falleth
  The light of truth sublime,
And gallant souls are faithful
  In this dark, traitorous time.
Still hearts are found that glory
  In God's good Word alone—
That will not sell their birthright,
  Nor foreign despot own.

Oh ! shut the gates on error !
Oh ! shut the gates on wrong !
Oh ! cling to your King's honour,
And in meek prayer be strong !
Watch where the wily Tempter
Bids parley with the foe ;
Watch where he thinks to enter,
And firmly answer—No !

THE HOLY LAND.

I HAVE a vision of the Holy Land,
And thus it visits me, that vision blest !
Not with crusaders streaming o'er its strand,
Or vain ambition's quest.

But o'er the mad world's hurrying to and fro,
Its brazen fair, its false claims to be wise,
I hear a whisper like the rose's blow—
" With Me in paradise !"

When heart and flesh are failing, yet the care
They still must take for present need, doth speak—
Before me rises soft an Outline fair,
And I no more am weak.

When scoffs the Greek, and infidels assume,
And Judas barters Heaven again for dross—
And (as in earth's one hour of dreadest gloom)
They mock, before the Cross !

Oh then uplifted, pleading for the world,
Methinks I see a dear, once wounded Hand !
In far-off vision Satan hence is hurled—
I see the Holy Land.

There is no sin, no pang, no sickness more—
What re-assemblings, claspings, gatherings sweet !
What meetings, and for ever, darkness o'er,
Beneath my Saviour's feet !

THE GUEST-CHAMBER.

WHERESOEVER I shall enter—little recks it where! the centre
 Of eternal life and glory is where'er my Saviour stands!
To my loneliest need He bendeth—all my hidden aching tendeth,
 Speaketh (wondrously forgiving!) of His Home in unseen Lands!

In my soul rise chambers holy—they were glorious, they were
 lowly;
 They were bright with love's dear vision—clasp and smile and
 converse fond!
Rooms of holy pain and weakness, shaded rooms of saintly
 meekness —
 Death himself a guest there only—love-sent from the Land
 beyond.

Ah no other chambers ever here below can match them! Never
 Can the forms belovéd furnish with their glory, this world's
 room!
Hush, my heart! as tears flow faster, listen, listen to the Master!
 Can there be, in His kind Presence, any homeless heart-sick
 gloom?

Think upon that wondrous story, how thy Lord, the King of Glory,
 In the world He stooped to ransom, had not where to lay His
 head!
Hiring from His household servant, who responded glad and fervent,
 One Guest Chamber, where He hallowed for us all, that Wine,
 that Bread!

Dost thou faint as years roll slowly, thinking in thy station lowly,
 It is long till that last Chamber other hands for me shall delve?
Waiting souls can serve the Master! prayer can make the hours fly
 faster.
He shall come again at evening, as He once came with the Twelve!

Hark, He sayeth, O He sayeth that which all our fear allayeth!
 "Let not your deep heart be troubled! I PREPARE a place for
 you!"
Let us be but guests, if only guests of Thine! for never lonely
 Wilt Thou leave us! Thou hast suffered all for us! Thy Word is
 true.

John Wilson Montgomery.

THE subject of this sketch has been for the last twenty-one years Clerk of the Downpatrick Poor-law Union. He was born at Billis, near Virginia, Co. Cavan, in the year 1834. His ancestors were Scotch settlers who came to that County in the wake of Baron Farnham.

Mr. Montgomery's early school life was passed at the Billis day school, then taught by an estimable man named Elliott. Afterwards he was for a number of years at Lisnagirl, another good school near Bailieborough, on the Farnham Estate. It was here the youth first discovered that he could make verse. The teacher was a Mr. Phair, a good man and a classical scholar, and took a deep interest in his boys. Mr. Montgomery was at this school until he became the oldest and the biggest boy in attendance. He was now looked upon by the principal not as a pupil, but as an assistant and friend. Mr. Phair had many tuitions in the neighbourhood, some of which took him away during school hours, and then the responsibility as well as the honour of substitute-principal fell to the lot of the youthful poet, and some of the incidents which happened on these occasions are still fresh in his memory. He left this school with a sound commercial education, as well as some knowledge of classics. In the meantime he had been learning shorthand with a view to an appointment on the Press. About this time Dr. Henry Montgomery, of Ballyjamesduff, volunteered to assist the poet to a position in his own profession, but the death of the young man's father changed the current of events for a time. Dr. Montgomery, also,

within a short period left the neighbourhood. He became
smitten with the Australian gold fever, gave up a lucrative
practice, and emigrated to that colony, where he succeeded
in amassing considerable wealth.

In the year 1856, when our author was just twenty-
two years of age, he was appointed Master of Bailieborough
Union Workhouse. He had been in the habit of writing
occasional poems for some time previous, and now that he
was in a fixed position and duties not too onerous, he
became a regular contributor to the two nearest newspapers, the "Meath Herald" and the "Cavan Observer."
He was encouraged in his literary pursuits by the Chair-
man of the Board, Sir John Young (afterwards Lord
Lisgar), who gave him the run of his library, and in many
another way showed his friendship. Mr. Montgomery
was now thoroughly recognised as the Bailieborough
poet, and the merit of his writings did not escape the
notice of his poetical brethren, for David Herbison, Bard
of Dunclug, alludes to him in one of his volumes as "the
sweet bard of Bailieborough." In 1859 Mr. Montgomery
first issued a collection of his poems under the title of
"Occasional Poems," and it is needless to say they were
inscribed to Sir John Young. In the year 1872 he
received his present appointment in Downpatrick, and as
was his wont became a contributor to the nearest newspaper—in this case the "Down Recorder." In 1877 he
collected another volume entitled "Rhymes Ulidian,"
inscribed to Mr. and Mrs. S. C. Hall, so long and so
favourably known in the world of literature. Mr.
Montgomery continued to occupy his leisure time in
describing the surrounding places of interest in verse.
These were published from time to time in the "Northern
Whig," "Belfast News-Letter," and "Down Recorder,"

and a further collection was published in 1887 under the title of "Fireside Lyrics," the preface of which was written by the late Mr. S. C. Hall immediately before his death. In it Mr. Hall speaks very highly, not only of the poems, but of the poet, as his friend; and in one of Mr. Hall's own prose works he expresses the thanks due to Mr. Montgomery for the services he had rendered in describing Irish scenery. During Mr. Montgomery's career he has made the acquaintance of a great many men of letters, his kindly disposition and sympathetic nature gaining him the esteem and respect of all with whom he comes in contact.

The following pieces are from "Fireside Lyrics," and the "Prelude" to that volume is so modestly descriptive of the author's reasons for writing poetry that we cannot forbear to quote it. Every poet will endorse the sentiment it contains :—

"FRESH fish from Helicon! who'll buy, who'll buy!"
O, Solomon, thou Solon of thy day,
Say is it sinful books to multiply,
   Or may voluminous rhymster write away?

Our presses choked with files of worthless stuff,
   All books of verse completely under ban;
Well may the reader cry out, "hold!"—"enough!"
   "How could'st thou write again, thou silly man?"

Well, I shall tell you how I came to write,
   And piecemeal thus produce another book!—
Was I to sit there glumly, night by night,
   Like some daft creature whom the muse forsook?

Whilst thought ranged up and down and round about,
   Alive to all that moved the stirring crowd;
Whilst marriage-bells, or bells of death rung out,
   I, moved by happiness, or sorrow-bowed;

Was I to sit there silent as the grave,
  And hear my comrades cheering in the race ?
The fear of man, I said, becomes a slave,
  Let Nature's children harp in boundless space.

The " cawing rooks, and kites that swim sublime,
  " In still repeated circles screaming loud"
In freedom glorious spend their span of time,
  Regardless of the strictures of the crowd.

And I ?—was I to mope, nor dare to sing,
  Lest some pert censor should condemn my voice ?
I will arise, I said, give fancy wing,
  And, fearless of the world, like bird, rejoice.

So chide not rashly, if impelled to write,
  One gives another volume to the press ;
Where one's inclinings lead towards bardic flight
  Make large allowance !—there is still redress !

Thou, gentle reader, need'st not largely buy,
  Or, having purchased, may assuage thine ire
By throwing book on cobweb shelf to lie,
  Or, should it merit worse—why in the fire.

KINGSFIELD.

I will sing you a song of the fields,
  Where nature at leisure reposes ;
Of a garden enclosure that yields
  Rich fruit and a million of roses ;
Nor yet are we far from town,
  While round us the twilight is stealing,
We can hear the sweet bells of old Down,
  Their notes o'er the meadow-lands pealing.

I will sing you a song of the dells,
  Where youth free of care freely rambles ;
Where nectar is drawn from the wells,
  And food may be plucked from the brambles.

Ye citymen, gas-blind and grey,
　Come out to the fields and be cheery,
Disporting like lambkins at play,
　Or slumbering contented when weary.

I will sing you a song of the trees,
　A melody runs in their numbers ;—
Not threatening, like winter-lashed seas,
　We hear it at night in our slumbers.
All softly they whisper of God,
　Or swell into high jubilation,
As when first upon Eden's pure sod
　They chanted the hymn of creation.

O, sing away musical boughs,
　At twilight and on to the morning,
When shrill chanticleer will arouse
　With Phœbus the hill-tops adorning;
And workmen with waggon or wain,
　By prospects of good day invited,
Will stride forth to garner the grain,
　Not weary of work, but delighted.

SNOWDROPS.

FRESH snowdrops pulled for me by kindly Jack !
　The child of her of earlier " snowdrop" lay ;
The precious gems recall my memory back
　To days long past, and scenes now far away.

O, cheery Spring !　O, lovely hedgerow bloom !
　And pearly flowerets pranking garden walk !
O beauteous world, and all devoid of gloom
　To those who with great Nature live and talk.

To those who watch the seasons as they pass,
　Who hear in rocks and trees and streams a voice,
Who see in trifles – e'en in blades of grass –
　The Master's hand, and in His works rejoice.

Great bards have sung the snowdrop, spotless gem,
  Soul-gifted songsters, now away from earth!
And my brief years are passing soon like them,
  I also go to pass a higher birth.

To spirit-life, believed in, though unseen,
  And far removed from this terrestrial ball:
Tho' clouds of darkness sometimes roll between
  That land and us, faith triumphs over all.

Believe in God, my child, and keep His law,
  And faithful walk according to thy light;
Then mayest thou rich consolation draw
  From birds and trees and flowers—from day and night.

From seasons sequent and the scenes they bring,
  Observing all, submit to one control;
The great, the small—those tiny flowers of spring
  Are part and parcel of the wond'rous whole.

The realms of Him who made these countless spheres,
  And set their courses—each in circuit bound;
Who knows no change—Who through a million years
  Is still the same—the Mighty! the Profound!

FRANCES RIDLEY HAVERGAL.

THY day was early spent. This world of woe
  Was not thy home; and thou wast called away;
  O strong of heart and cultured in thy lay,
We scarce can write, our tears so freely flow!

Gone the fair songstress whom our souls admired,
  Gone the sweet Christian poet of the age;
  We turn with awe the uncompleted page,
And low before the lyrist heaven-inspired.

A flood of light illumed the dark cold earth,
  Wherever thou in song didst lead the way;

The merest tyro caught the golden ray,
And rendered homage for thy glorious birth.

Beyond the reach of strugglers in the race,
  No envy reigned when thou didst strike the lyre;
  But all united in one grand desire
To yield thee—what was clearly thine—first place.

O brilliant worker in the cause of God!
  Who takes thy place as leader of our song?
  We wander blindly through the lisping throng,
And weep, but faint not, 'neath the chastening rod.

Great is the Lord, and wond'rous in His ways;
  He gives to us the sunshine and the rain;—
  'Tis ours to take the pleasure and the pain,
In weal or woe, still shouting songs of praise.

The Lord is great, let all the earth obey,
  Tell of His goodness every living thing;
  From founts perennial bounteous mercies spring;
And earthly losses may not dim the way.

Hope built upon the Lord can know no blight;
  His glories shine around the trusting soul;
  'Tis He who made those orbs that round us roll,
And, mightier than all, the great sun's light.

The Lord is love; and other minstrels strong
  Are sure to rise to charm the Christian world,
  As Heber, Hemans, Havergal unfurl'd,
And bore the banner through the fields of song.

S. K. Cowan, M.A.

MAJOR SAMUEL KENNEDY COWAN, M.A., is
an officer in the Third Royal Irish Rifles, and resides
at Dunmurry, a beautiful suburban district of the City of
Belfast. He was born at Grove Green, near Lisburn, on
13th August, 1850, and is the son of Andrew Cowan, Esq.,
J.P., Barrister-at-Law (B.A., T.C.D.), of Ballylintagh
House, Hillsborough, Co. Down. He is also great
grandson of Captain Andrew Cowan, who, during the
Irish Rebellion, raised a company of sturdy yeomen from
the tenants of his own estate to assist the Government,
and afterwards proceeded with them to India to reinforce
the troops there, and was granted a captaincy in the
101st Regiment (the Bengal Fusiliers) in recognition of
his services. His paternal grandmother was a poetess of
note, and published a volume of exceptional merit. His
mother also wrote some lyrics of much excellence. It
will, therefore, be seen that Major Cowan is the descendant
of an ancestry noted in the field of literature as well as
for courage and daring.

The first school of importance to which he was sent
was at West Cowes, Isle of Wight. Here he first imbibed
his passion for the sea, and was one of the crew of the
school lifeboat at the age of twelve years. In his thir-
teenth year he was sent to Edward the Sixth's Grammar
School, Bromsgrove, Worcestershire, of which Dr. Collis,
one of the first Hebrew scholars of his day, was head
master. Here he was always first in his Greek and Latin
verse composition, and before he left the school was without a rival in that department. He afterwards entered

Trinity College, Dublin, and here he first became known
to the public as a poet. His tutor accidentally came
across some of his fugitive verses, and at once perceived
their unmistakable merit. He induced Mr. Cowan to
write for "Kottabos," the college magazine. About the
same time he submitted some of his lyrics to Mr. Alfred
S. Gatty, the great musical composer, who forwarded him
a cheque for two guineas for "The Old Sweet Story,"
accompanied by a letter in which he said, "You have
exceptional powers as a lyrist, and I thoroughly advise
you to adopt literature as a profession." Mr. Gatty
afterwards set this song to music for Miss Edith Wynne,
and it is now a very popular song. After a distinguished
career at Trinity College, including classical honours,
Mr. Cowan obtained his B.A. degree in 1871, and
M.A. in 1874. He now became a very prolific
writer, and the enthusiasm with which his new
songs and recitations were received by musicians and
elocutionists was unbounded. There is scarcely a modern
edition of any standard work on elocution in the United
Kingdom that does not contain one of his recitations ;
and some of his pieces, such as "Becalmed," "In the Old
Canteen," and "Round the Bivouac Fire," are of world-
wide reputation.

It would be impossible for us in the space at our
disposal to give in detail the multitude of works of which
Mr. Cowan is author. He writes fine-art verses for twelve
London firms, and these to the extent of about five hundred
annually. He is author of about fifty booklets for birth-
day, Christmas, and other gifts. He is a regular contributor to "The Girl's Own Paper," "Sunday at Home,"
"The Theatre Magazine," "Little Folks," "Judy," "Irish
Household Gazette," and many other publications.

Among the books to which he has contributed compositions may be mentioned " Readings from British Authors" (Carson Bros.), " Poets at Play" (Eyre & Spottiswoode), "Baynham's Select Reader (Blackie & Son), " Garry's Elocutionist " (M. Ward), " The Household Library of Irish Poets " (New York), " The Modern Elocutionist," "Forde's Elocutionist," and a number of others, throughout Great Britain and the Colonies.

Mr. Cowan first collected his poetical pieces in the year 1872, under the simple title " Poems," and in 1879 "The Murmur of .the Shells." These were followed by " A Broken Silence" in 1883. Of this work a critic remarks : " His verses abound in rich descriptive talent, and gives evidence of a careful study of the works of some of our best known poetical writers of modern days." In 1884 he issued a little work entitled "Play," and in the following year " Fancies in Feathers." This work is intended for children chiefly, but is of interest to all lovers of simple and sweetly-flowing musical verse. The subjects of the poems are birds, and, considering such common-place themes, there is a gracefulness of fancy and delicacy of feeling that are truly refreshing. In 1886 "Laurel Leaves " was published, and "Jemima Jinkings and other Jingles" in 1892. His latest work, "Roses and Rue," was published in 1893, and was quite up to the best of his previous productions.

As a test of the favour with which Mr. Cowan's lyrics have been greeted, it may be stated that over one hundred of them have been set to music by the very foremost English composers, and many of them have become exceedingly popular, such as " Out on the Deep " (Foli's great song), " Just Because " (Pinsuti), " Old Love-letters " (Sir A. Sullivan), " The Crusader " (Bonheur), " Anchored," &c.

A few years ago, when Mrs. Mona Caird's discussion on "Is Marriage a Failure" was rife, Mr. Cowan wrote a little *brochure* on the subject, in comic verse, for Mr. Thomas, London, and 15,000 copies were sold inside three weeks. In 1892 Mr. Cowan was selected by the "Three Irish Sisters" to compose the *In Memoriam* poem on the Duke of Clarence. He also composed "Farewell to Erin" (set to music by R. F. Harvey) for Madame Titiens on her last departure from Ireland to America. She sung it at Queenstown before leaving amid great enthusiasm.

As might be expected this pleasing poet is a great favourite at entertainments and in society generally. He admires unstudied manners, and looks with suspicion on the icy conventionalities of etiquette. He delights in the sea, and his taste in this direction is embodied in many of his poems. Long may he revel in the beauties of nature and be a source of delight to others by his glowing descriptions of them.

A BOUQUET OF FLOWERS.

A BOUQUET of cherished flowers
I gathered one Summer's day ;
And some of them still are blooming,
But others have faded away.

Have faded for ever and ever—
Frail flowers that I could not save :
But my thoughts still linger with them,
Like flowers upon their grave.

And I know as the hours fly forward,
With their changing lights and shades,
My flowers will sere and wither
Till my whole fair bouquet fades.

And I think, in the world's wide garden
 Of myriad minds and men,
How like are the friends I cherish
 To the bouquet I gathered then !

A few true friends in sunshine ;
 A few tried friends in tears ;
A wreath of roses and cypress—
 A bouquet of bygone years !

A few of my flowers have faded,
 But I know they shall live again,
And bloom out of Death's dark shadow,
 As a rainbow blooms out of rain.

And I know as the years fly forward,
 . And wither the world's bright dells,
We shall bloom, as of old, together—
 A bouquet of Immortelles !

THE CHILDREN'S FRIEND.

THERE is a foot that falleth
 Low on the nursery stair,
And a pallid hand that passeth
 Over the children's hair.
Over their shining tresses,
 As they sing and prattle at play ;
And the pallid hand is evermore
 Stealing the gold away.

And when the children slumber,
 Softly anear it slips,
And, bending low, in the still shadow,
 Kisses the rosebud lips ;
Then slowly the rose-hues leave them,
 And slowly the fragrant breath,
Till the rosy lips of life are changed
 To the pallid lilies of Death.

Ah, mourn not, fading children!
  For a life that waxeth cold;
For sweet is Death, who gathereth
  Your roses and your gold!
He would not leave your glories
  To fade beneath the sod,
But hath gathered your flowers for the bowers of heaven,
  And your gold for the jewels of God!

BECALMED.

IT was as calm, as calm could be,
  A death-still night, in June;
A silver sail, on a silver sea,
  Under a silver moon.

Not a breath of air the still sea stirred;
  But all on the dreaming deep
The white ship lay, like a white sea bird,
  With folded wings, asleep.

For a long, long month, not a breath of air!
  For a month not a drop of rain!
And the gaunt crew watched in wild despair,
  With a fever in throat and brain.

And they saw the shore, like a dim cloud, stand
  On the far horizon sea;
It was only a day's short sail to the land,
  And the haven where they would be!

Too faint to row; no signal brought
  An answer far or nigh;
Father! have mercy; leave them not
  Alone on the deep to die.

And the gaunt crew prayed on the decks above,
  And the women prayed below:
" One drop of rain, for Heaven's great love!
  O God, for a breeze to blow!"

But never a shower from the skies would burst,
    And never a breeze would come ;
Ah, Christ ! to think that man can thirst,
    And starve, in sight of home !

But out to sea, with the drifting tide,
    The vessel drifted away ;
Till the far-off shore, like the dim cloud, died,
    And the wild crew ceased to pray.

Like fiends they glared, with their eyes aglow ;
    Like beasts, with hunger wild ;
But a mother knelt in the cabin below,
    By the bed of her little child.

It slept, and lo ! in its sleep it smiled,
    A babe of summers three ;
" O Father, save my little child,
    Whatever comes to me !"

Calm gleamed the sea ; calm gleamed the sky ;
    No cloud—no sail—in view ;
And they cast them lots for who should die
    To feed the starving crew.

Like beasts they glared, with hunger wild,
    And their red, glazed eyes aglow ;
And the death-lot fell on the little child
    That slept in the cabin below !

And the mother shrieked in wild despair—
    "O God ! my child, my son !
They will take his life ; it is hard to bear—
    Yet, Father, Thy will be done !

And she waked the child from its happy sleep,
    And she knelt by the cradle bed :
" We thirst, my child, on the lonely deep—
    We are dying, my child, for bread.

On the lone, lone sea no sail—no breeze—
  Not a drop of rain in the sky ;
We thirst—we starve on the lonely seas,
  And thou, my child, must die !"

She wept ; what tears her wild soul shed
  Not I, but God, knows best.
And the child rose up from its cradle bed
  And crossed its hands on its breast.   .

" Father," he lisped, " so good—so kind,
  Have pity on mother's pain ;
For mother's sake, a little wind —
  Father, a little rain !"

And she heard them shout for the child from the deck,
  And she knelt on the cabin stairs :
"The child ! the child !" they cry, " Stand back,
  And a curse on your idiot prayers !"

And the mother rose in her wild despair,
  And she bared her throat to the knife :
" Strike—strike—me—me ; but spare, O spare
  My child—my dear son's life !"

O God ! it was a ghastly sight—
  Red eyes, like flaring brands,
And a hundred belt-knives flashing bright
  In the clutch of skeleton hands !

" Me—me—strike—strike, ye fiends of death !"
  But soft, thro' the ghastly air,
Whose falling tear was that ?   Whose breath
  Waves thro' the mother's hair ?

A flutter of sail—a ripple of seas—
  A speck on the cabin pane ;
O God, it is a breeze—a breeze—
  And a drop of blesséd rain !

And the mother rushed to the cabin below,
    And she wept on the babe's bright hair :
" The sweet rain falls—the sweet winds blow ;
    Father has heard thy prayer !"

But the child has fallen asleep again ;
    And lo ! in its sleep it smiled :
" Thank God !" she cried, " for His wind and His rain ;
    Thank God for my little child !"

William J. Gallagher.

MR. WILLIAM JOSEPH GALLAGHER is a young
poet of great hope and promise. He was born at
Rylands, County Donegal, in the year 1864. He
was educated at Ardagh National School under Mr.
Rutherford, of whom he speaks in terms of the highest
praise. After leaving school, he continued to keep up his
acquaintance with books by reading the works of some of
the great English poets, being particularly fond of Shelly,
Wordsworth, and Byron. In course of time he connected
himself with the "literary circle" of the *Weekly Irish
Times*, and was successful several times at the competi-
tions for prizes offered by the editor. He afterwards
wrote poems and prose sketches for *Chambers' Journal* and
Old and Young. He still contributes to these publications,
and takes a lively interest in the competition column of
the *Belfast Weekly News*, where such eminent poets as
Major Cowan and Miss Knox are among his competitors.

The readers of Irish literature may expect to hear
more of this young poet in the near future.

A NEW YEAR REFLECTION.

QUICKLY passing are the seasons,
    Hours and days and weeks go by ;
No one dares to ask for reasons
    Of our laugh, or of our sigh.
Dream an hour or dream forever,
    Time will slide its even course,
But the great Almighty giver
    Never gave to one remorse.

Every joy there is in living
    Comes from working night and day,
Something new for earth achieving,
    Seeking still to shed a ray
On the path of some lone creature
    Who less fortunate may be—
Just alike in form and feature,
    But the prey of misery.

To the heart thus filled with duty
    And a sense of bliss enjoyed,
Earth has radiant glowing beauty;
    Life contains no empty void.
Heads of planning, hands of healing,
    Feet that move on mercy bent,
These will merit holy feeling—
    Not in vain such lives are spent.

All can hear the bell's loud clangour—
    All can sing, if but they will;
But the idle sighs with langour,
    While the worker has a thrill,
Full of earnest joys that linger
    Till the last dim niche is reached,
When the hearer and the singer
    Need no more a sermon preached.

Ring, ye bells! laugh loud, ye maidens!
    Joyous be ye, boys and girls!

Richest treasure is your cadence,
    Rippling soft like wavelet's curls.
Join the hearty chorus greeting,
    Friend and foe for once to-day;
There may come another meeting,
    But the wish may be away.

Holy season! when at parting
    Of the ways we stand in thought,
Memories sweet and sad upstarting
    With so many New Years fraught—
Oh, just now, whate'er your station,
    Join the throng, let mirth have sway!
Clasp each hand in emulation,
    Wish each other joy to-day.

AN IVIED LAY.

A GAY yet sombre spot I know,
    Where tendrils of the ivy twine;
A shelter from the winter's snow—
    A shadow in the summer's shine.
That spot looks dark; the mouldy stones,
    Between the stems, are hoar and grey;
The wind behind the wall now moans,
    Then whistles in a dreamy way!

'Tis hard to tell which mood would fit
    By which to view a spot like this;
In deep despondency to sit,
    Or dream, ecstatic, full of bliss!
At any time the ivy view,
    In which deep tints of green appear;
Its richness and its glossy hue
    Speak cheerful of a higher sphere.

Another charm it hath; my heart
    Would thus deep trusting cling to friend—

Each unto each a counterpart,
　　Each working to a common end.
And large and hopeful in our trust
　　Grow old and grey, yet never pall !
Although upon us grow Time's rust,
　　Our firm resolve as one to fall !

Within my heart there is a place
　　Where gloom and sunshine mingled lie ;
Dark boughs of doubt each other lace,
　　Until I seek a purer sky—
The sky of trust, serene and fair,
　　In it all forms so lovely see,
All glowing tints, both soft and rare,
　　Deep centred like the ivy tree.

'Tis strange how grows a common theme
　　Until it reaches heights sublime !
Some rust away, their life a dream—
　　Some triumph o'er the wrecks of Time !
The ivy mirrors proudest hope
　　That shines above a ruined dome—
A mighty thing that well can ope
　　The gates to Heaven, Peace, and Home.

Nicholas Daly.

MR. NICHOLAS DALY is a native of the County Cork. He was born in the village of Killavullen, in that county, about the year 1863. From his childhood he had a great taste for Art. At the age of nine years his imitation of copperplate writing could scarcely be distinguished from the copy. At the age of twelve his parents removed to the city of Cork, and the youth was sent to the North Monastery School. Here he was distinguished for his writing and English composition. When parties were shown specimens of his penmanship and told who executed it, some were so incredulous as to seek out the writer in order to allay their curiosity and see the statement verified. Messrs. John Mitchell and John Martin once visited the school, and of course were shown the writing. They looked on with interest while Mr. Daly wrote a few pages which to their great delight he presented them with.

On leaving school about the age of fifteen he went to learn the trade of carpenter, and in the capacity of foreman in Dublin and Cork he has executed many a work of importance. A short time ago he entered an architect's office as draughtsman but soon tired of this and received an appointment as clerk of works which he still continues to hold. Mr. Daly attended the School of Art for some years, and his study of this branch has been attended with very marked success, for to-day Mr. Daly's name as an artist is far beyond the city of Cork. As an illuminator of addresses he is in great request, and the Press notices of his work in this department are extremely flattering. The following notice from a daily paper of an address presented to Mr. John E. Redmond, some time ago, is a fair specimen of public opinion :—" The artist is Mr. Daly. The address is inscribed on a coloured ground in the centre, and around it is a scroll which for beauty of design and artistic execution could not be surpassed. The design is entirely original, as is the initial letter of the address which is exceedingly fine. Mr. Daly deserves to be congratulated for his splendid piece of work whose artistic merit cannot be awarded too much praise."

Mr. Daly has written poetry ever since his schoolboy days, but he is now best known by the volume which he published in 1893, entitled "Upbraid not Eve." It is an allegorical poem, and is a powerful defence of our first parent Eve. Its object is to show that if ordinary mortals of the present day were in a similar position they would just act as she did. It represents a mortal embittered by cares, after having assailed his first parent with being the cause of all his miseries, sinks into a deep sleep, and fancies he is honoured by a celestial visitant who gives him wings and leads him beyond earth's influence to a most beautiful planet, and confers on him the unique privilege of enjoying the magnificence of its scenery for an unlimited period, with power to change the scienic splendour at his will, upon the condition that nothing earthly should alter his sympathies henceforth. The following selection represents what the celestial host said to his supremely happy guest when they arrived on the beautiful planet :—

> Then spoke that mystic being grand :—
> " Sublimely-favoured mortal lowly,
> Know'st thou this bright and happy land
> Was formed for thee, thus pure and holy ?

Those lovely vales—those spicy bowers—
 Those hills in azure distance looming—
Those brilliant shores with fadeless flowers
 Luxuriant on their margins blooming ;—
Those lakes of liquid pearl where swell
 Those amber sails in floating splendour ;
Those ivory mansions bright, where dwell
 Those Spirits fair, in friendship tender ;
Those gentle gales, that waft along
 The odours sweet of various flowers,
With angels' voices, sweet in song,
 From full a thousand tuneful bowers :
This glorious world, by circling light
 Peculiar zoned—this floating Heaven,,
With mantling blooms, superb bedight —
 Is thine—with strange injunction given."

" Here may'st thou dwell for evermore,
 Presiding o'er those bright dominions,
Profuse endowed with spirit-lore,
 And furnished fair with spirit-pinions ;
But, far removed for aye must be
 Thy ardent zeal for earthly pleasure,
And aught terrestrial, dear to thee,
 Henceforth be deemed *mistaken treasure*."

" Here, myriad million years may fly
 As sweetly as the transient hours
Thou oft hast spent in dalliance high,
 And love, 'mid Erin's emerald bowers.
And should those scenes celestial, fail
 Through lack of change to charm incessant,
Seek thou yon arboretted vale,
 Where fountains flew of gold liquescent,
Where thou wilt find a gentle knoll,
 Grotesque with myriad perforations,
Through which in wreathed volumes, roll
 Bright odorif'rous exhalations ;

Around its base, in feathery fold,
   And gay festoon, bright shrubs are braided
Which, twining gay round trellissed gold,
   A grotto form, all sweetly shaded,
Whose portal nestles, nigh-concealed,
   By dangling wreaths of damasked flowers,
Wherein 'mid shadows, dim-revealed,
   By sprayey fountains' sparkling showers,
A *pillar* stands on floor of pearl,
   Of alabaster, golden-fluted,
With massive base of moulded beryl,
   And flowered cornelian cap, voluted,
On which an *opal tablet* rests,
   In faint refulgence sweetly beaming,
Whereon thou'lt letter thy requests—
   Thy pencil be thy pinion gleaming;
From thence, short time, I weet, will fly,
   Ere thou wilt view·a transformation,
From eminence sublimely high,
   Thy safe and self-selected station."

" Now—fare-thee-well—may'st thou for aye
   Enjoy this sphere of hallow'd beauty,
Content to dwell from earth away
   And aught of earth—be still thy duty
Which, if transgressed, with lightning's flight,
   Relentless back thou shalt be taken,
And as from dreams of worlds of light,
   Thy slumb'ring form on earth shall waken."

Thus spoke that mystic being grand,
   With smiles his glowing face adorning,
Extending high his radiant hand,
   As though t' impress his friendly warning.
Then, as beneath the torrid ray,
   With tepid waves of peaceful motion,
An iceberg melts unseen away
   Into the vast and liquid ocean,

Thus—mingling with ethereal space,
That form to viewless essence vanished,
Assured the splendours of the place,
All earthly, from my soul had banished.

KILLAVULLEN.

(MY NATIVE VILLAGE.)

THE river deep, the sombre hill,
The sheltered chapel, and the mill,
The lawn, where flowed the lovely rill
　　Through alder branches waving.

The rugged rocks, with many a cave,
Responsive to each winding wave
That through the litchened chambers rave,
　　Their walls fantastic laving.

The graveyard green, the abbey old,
Enrobed in trembling ivied fold,
The fairy courts, where we are told
　　Such power melodious lingers.

The sable sluice, the bright cascade,
Where varied lights prismatic played,
The castles old, to ruin laid
　　By Time's defacing fingers.

The ancient limekilns quaint and brown
That o'er the plains dismantled frown,
And mar the sunlight streaming down
　　Through many a bright embrazure.

The gray lagoon, the glassy pond,
The pine-groves stretching far beyond,
The hills that bound my vision fond
　　With dreamy hues of azure.

The lovely village, fair to view,
'Neath circling wreaths of smoky blue,
The cottage where my childhood grew
    With sacred love regarded.

The group who nightly sought its hearth
For converse sweet and homely mirth,
Who prized a hero's precious worth,
    And craven hearts discarded.

The soggarth's cave 'mid greenwood dells,
The orchards gay, the holy wells,
O'er which delightful memory dwells—
    Those loved retreats of childhood.

For ever to my fancy's eye,
In mirrored truth extended lie,
While quaint traditions sanctify
    Each emerald vale and wildwood.

One feature lone sublime appears,
Unloved 'mid scenes of youthhood's years,
The home of unforgotten fears—
    The schoolhouse darkly towering.

A teacher there for many a day
Relentless ruled with awful sway;
Sad fancies oft his form portray,
    And features grimly lowering.

But passed is now his vain career
That claims not one pathetic tear,
Though gentler natures marvel here
    The course uncouth he wended.

While those who cowered before his nod,
And trembled 'neath his lifted rod,
Full many a walk of life have trod,
    By many a fate attended.

Those figures—lithesome as the fawn
Careering o'er the mossy lawn—
Are from those scenes for aye withdrawn,
    Though linked by memory ever.

Some now are scattered far and wide
Beyond the ocean's misty tide,
And more—their graves hermetic hide
    For ever and for ever.

God grant, when we shall meet again
On Josaphet's extended plain,
At God's right hand, with joy amain,
    Secure from fears infernal.

Not one of all that glorious band
Will missing be, but hand in hand,
With our old master shining stand
    In joy and love eternal.

Joseph A. Latimer.

MR. JOSEPH A. LATIMER was born on the 9th
April, 1867, at Ballybofey, Co. Donegal. He
received the usual education afforded by the
national schools of the district. As he grew up he
acquired a taste for military life, and at the age of nineteen
he joined the force of the Royal Irish Constabulary.
Here he felt constrained to study more than posture and
muscular development. To his military duties he added
the cultivation of the muse and the study of current
literature. Although he had composed verse from his
schooldays, it was not until 1887 that Mr. Latimer commenced to publish his songs. They first appeared in the

Weekly Irish Times, an organ whose editor has done so much to foster and encourage native genius. Since then he has been a constant contributor. His lyrics have attracted considerable attention, and he frequently receives application to reprint them. Evidently his songs have found an echo in the heart of many a wooer of the muse, for it is no uncommon thing to see a sonnet in praise of them in the columns of the weekly newspapers. His songs are much in request by musicians, and many of them have been set to music and the copyright of them purchased. Among the most popular of them may be mentioned " The Sweet Moyola," and " The Old Clock," both of which have been set to music by Mr. Fred. Horan, organist of Christ Church, Dublin, and published by Messrs Boosey & Co. ; " No, No," which gained a prize at the humorous competition of the *Weekly Irish Times* in 1890, and " My Grandmother's Spinning-wheel."

Mr. Latimer has written a great deal of sweet lyric poetry, though he has never issued a collection of his works. It is to be hoped that ere long his poems will be found in a form more accessible to the public than the back numbers of a newspaper.

WHAT IS LIFE ?

WHAT is life ? A passing shadow
　Fleeting o'er the sands of time,
Swiftly dying, soon forgotten,
　Like the echo of a chime.
As a ripple of the ocean
　Breaks in foam upon the strand ;
As the waters wildly raging
　After storm are soon becalmed.

What is life ?   'Tis but a picture
    Swiftly passing out of sight,
Leaving but a dim remembrance
    Like a vision of the night.
Giving us ecstatic pleasure,
    Giving us exquisite pain ;
But forgotten in the morning
    Like a phantom of the brain.

What is life ?   A chord of music
    Dying swiftly on the air,
Leaving but a slight vibration
    To remind us it was there ;
As a cloud on the horizon
    Is dissolved before the wind,
As the winter snows are melted
    Leaving not a trace behind.

What is life ?   A lone spark flickering
    Momentarily, then is dead,
Like a little pearly raindrop
    On a burning desert shed ;
As a blossom in the summer
    First will flourish, then decay,
So it is predestinated
    Life will fastly fade away.

What is life ?   'Tis the aurora
    That illumes the polar night,
Fading quickly, leaving darkness
    Where its streamers shone so bright.
As a short-lived radiant meteor
    Through the sky will swiftly pass,
Life is surely " but a vapour,"
    And we wither as the grass.

AN IRISH DANCE.

POETS may sing in their classic lays
  Of the witching strains of the voiceful lyre,
Of the harp-notes woke by the Cymric bards
  To nerve their chiefs with the battle fire ;
But give me the notes of the mellow flute
  As through the welkin they softly steal,
With all the pleasure that they evoke
  In an Irish jig or a rousing reel.

Poets may sing in their varied tongues
  The intoxication of waltzes sweet,
How in spirit the dancers whirl and glide
  With a dreamy movement of forms and feet;
But give me an Irish lad and lass,
  In a barn where the flute's soft echoes peal,
As they merrily chase the flying hours
  In a lively jig or a rousing reel.

Give me the songs of my own dear land,
  Give me its manly pleasures too,
Give me the courage of its sons—
  Its graceful daughters, with hearts so true ;
And I'd rather the joys of one sweet hour
  Than any that other lands reveal,
To trip to the sound of the mellow flute
  In an Irish jig or a rousing reel.

THE WARRIOR'S RETURN.

UPON the rath the beacon fire
  Shot upwards with a ruddy flame ;
'Twas watched by many an ancient sire
  And many a careworn, anxious dame.
And answering fires on every height,
  A blazing line, shot from the coast,
Marked out the path with joyful light
  Of the returning warrior host.

A murmur rose, and gathered strength,
   Like " many waters" on the ear,
" They're coming, coming home at length,
   Father, son, brother, husband dear.
Our gallant king is at their head
   And trophies of the war they bear,
Then haste, the banquet tables spread,
   And for the feast and dance prepare.

The warrior denied by age
   Of joining the adventurous bands,
Stood on the hilltop with the sage,
   Eager to light the burning brands ;
The minstrel bent his silvered head
   As he composed a martial song,
And many a grateful tear was shed—
   A vent to feelings pent-up long.

When lo ! a presage of some ill,
   A portent of some evil dire,
The blazing lights on every hill
   In quick succession all expire ;
And borne upon the balmy gale,
   With terror that each bosom shared,
Like the low mournful banshee's wail,
   The warrior's sad *cavine* is heard.

The tramping feet sound in the glen,
   Emerging from the stern defile
Is seen the war-worn group of men
   Treading once more their native isle.
But oh ! what tidings, sad, they bring,
   The chanting Druids at their head,
In broken accents sadly sing
   The virtues of the fallen dead.

They sing how on the Alpine steeps
   The noble hero fought and fell ;

And heavier, deeper sadness creeps
Into the hearts that loved him well.
'Twas a black day, a heavy shade
O'ercast it, of the direst gloom,
When morning, martial clansmen laid
The royal Dathé in the tomb.

William Maxwell.

THE subject of this notice is a native of Co. Down, and was born in the year 1839. His parents belonged to the farming class, and were exemplary for their uprightness of principle and Christian piety. William was the eldest of the family, and received the early part of his education at the neighbouring school. He greatly enjoyed school life, and made rapid progress in the various branches of instruction. Although occasionally employed on the farm, no taste for farming seems to have developed itself, for at the age of fourteen, by his own request, he was apprenticed to a woollen-draper in a neighbouring town. In the course of about eighteen months, however, his employer retired from business, and the lad was obliged to return home, where he went to school again for a short time. Soon afterward he was employed as a substitute for a neighbouring teacher during his absence of some months. Here he acquired an interest in teaching, and a vacancy having occurred in a school a few miles distant, he offered himself as a candidate. After a competitive examination with several candidates all older than himself, he obtained the appointment, although then only in his seventeenth year. The teaching profession at that time did not offer much

inducement to a youth of talent and education, so in less
than two years he gave up the profession, and went to
Belfast to enter on a commercial life in the year 1857.

Two years afterward there was a great religious
awakening throughout the North of Ireland, and its
influence on Mr. Maxwell gave a new aim to his object in
life. His evenings were now occupied in evangelistic
work, and he was seized with a strong desire for the
moral and spiritual improvement of those whose condition
this kind of work made him familiar with. For several
years he continued his mercantile pursuits by day, and
employed his evenings in the endeavour to advance the
interests of religion, now and then moulding his thoughts
into verse, and sending them to the local newspapers.
About the year 1874 he resigned his situation, and became
an agent of the Belfast Town Mission, and in 1889 was
appointed to his present position as secretary and financial
agent for the same society.

For the last twenty-five years Mr. Maxwell has been
in the habit of expressing his thoughts more or less
frequently in verse. The subjects of his compositions are
to a large extent religious, and the bent of the author's
mind is evident in every one of them. They are written
with a purpose, and inspired by the loftiest motives. He
never attempts the higher flights of poetic fancy. He
does not write merely to please others. His object seems
to be more to improve than to please others. In his
efforts to do the one, however, he succeeds in doing both.
The products of his pen are pleasant as well as profitable
reading. There are many gems of thought in his
writings, and they are expressed in language which
everyone who reads can understand. With the exception
of an occasional *brochure*, Mr. Maxwell has not issued his

works in a collected form. It is to be hoped he will do so in the near future, as there is little doubt that from their high merit they would meet with a very general acceptance.

TIMES OF REFRESHING.

THE morning dawns—the shadows flee—
  The nearing clouds in blessing break ;
The Master comes—He calls for thee :
  Spouse of the Lamb, awake! awake !

To praise and prayer; to saintly life
  Arise in this auspicious hour ;
The valley full of bones is rife
  With signs of resurrection power.

O cease the unbelieving cry,
  "Our bones are dried, our hope is lost,"
While multitudes beneath Thine eye
  Start from the grave a marshalling host.

Footsteps divine are falling near ;
  The Master calls us to His feet :
To all besides we close the ear,
  And hasten to the mercy seat.

Had'st Thou been here, Almighty Lord,
  What buried souls had lived ere now !
But speak, O! speak the quickening word—
  The Life and Resurrection Thou.

Come from the winds, O vital breath !
  Descend and breathe upon the slain.
O come, thou Conqueror of death ;
  Possess our hearts, subdue and reign.

To anxious souls reveal the cross ;
  Apply the vitalizing balm ;
Till thousands sing, " He died for us,"
  And give the glory to the Lamb.

Witness of Jesus, Holy Ghost,
    With living faith our souls inspire :
Repeat once more the Pentecost
    And give the baptism of fire.

THE EVENING STAR—A CITY MUSING.

BEYOND the hills the sun has set ;
    And while the disappearing day,
With tinge of sadness and regret,
    Parts slowly from the West away,
Like solitary gem afar
Shines out the beauteous evening star.

Aweary with the ceaseless din,
    The busy toil and breathless haste,
And longing for the calm within
    That seems all broken or displaced ;
'Mid clanking hoof and thundering car
I bless the silent evening star.

In vain your glare, ye gaudy lights !
    What care I for your rival claims ?
Disdainful of these dazzling sights,
    And dead to their ambitious aims,
My spirits' rapt communings are
With yonder holy evening star !

No tumults vex her reign serene ;
    The storms have reverently retired :
Fair type of what our orb had been
    Had faithless man to Heaven aspired !
O when shall sin no longer mar
And earth be fair as evening star ?

Vouchsafe Thy Spirit's inward beam,
    O Thou who bid'st the Vesper shine :
Transport my all too grovelling dream
    Of things eternal and divine
Until the shadows flee afar,
Nor veil the " Bright and Morning Star."

STRONG DRINK'S APPEAL TO THE EYE.

FAIR to the eye! Ah me, how fair
  The fruit forbidden tempting hung!
As Satan wove his fatal snare
  Around the sinless world so young.
    'Tis thus by fascination still
    The arch-deceiver seeks to kill.

Behind the lavish gilt and glare
  Within that Bacchanalian shrine
The serpent lurks; his sting is there,
  Though all his scales like jewels shine:
    Fair to the eye the wine may flow,
    But death and doom lie coiled below.

The varied hues, the mirror bright,
  The radiance of that gorgeous bar,
Are but the wreckers' deadly light
  Displayed upon the rocks afar :
    Once let the ship but reach that shore,
    Who shall the drowning crew deplore?

Awake! ye sons of toil and know
  That dazzling sheen is but the snare
To make your poverty and woe
  Supply the tempter's sumptuous fare—
    The harvest of your sweat and pain
    Transformed to your betrayer's gain.

O! when shall righteous rage displace
  The power of Drink's bewitching spell—
Unmask the foul and hideous face
  Of this bedizened Jezebel :
    Dash from her brazen brow the crown,
    And to the pavement cast her down?

SPRING.

MY heart for the faded glory grieves,
   When the summer has passed away;
But oh! I joy for the opening leaves
   That sprinkle the boughs to-day,
As the Spring her emerald garland weaves
   For the fair young princess May.

How chill was the winter's shivering breath
   A few short weeks ago!
O, where is now the shadow of death,
   And the all-enshrouding snow?
Gone, gone! the freshening verdure saith,
   And the streamlet's dancing flow.

The Mayflower wakes to the brook's sweet song,
   While the violet, meek and shy,
Is fain to join with the primrose throng
   As they breathe their speechless joy;
While the soaring lark sings loud and long
   In the sapphire vault on high.

O, beauteous type; O, promise fair,
   In this drear vale of time,
Of the cloudless light and the balmy air
   In the far celestial clime,
And the never failing forces there
   Of life's immortal prime!

Our dead, all ripe as the autumn corn,
   Or fresh as the primrose bloom,
By the hand of a trusted Saviour borne
   To the seed-plot of the tomb,
Shall spring in the nearing deathless morn
   All glorious from the gloom.

O yes, 'tis coming, the fadeless Spring,
   And the never-withering flowers;
The ceaseless song, the tireless wing,
   And the sinless Eden bowers,
By the grace of Heaven's immortal King
   Through the endless ages ours.

Edith H. Coghlan.

MISS COGHLAN is a native of Cork, and was born at Lislee, Courtmacsherry, in that county. She is the elder daughter of Mr. Heber Coghlan from whom she inherits her love of literature. When she was four years old her mother died, and, as might be expected she became greatly attached to her father. He watched the development of her genius with great interest, and being himself a poet gave her every encouragement to carry out her literary aspirations. Although young in years she has contributed largely to current literature, and every reader of the Cork or Dublin weekly newspapers is familiar with her writings.

It is said of Sir Walter Scott that "even the dumb animals became happier in his presence." This fact has frequently been exemplified in the case of Miss Coghlan. Animals which have fled from others in terror have come to her to be fondled, and birds have left their favourite haunts to attend to her call, and partake of crumbs from her hand. Even the refractory jennet, which generally contrived to outwit some of the sterner sex, became gentle and tractable when under her control. She has a great love for pet dogs and birds, and is passionately fond of flowers. The garden forms one of her chief sources of recreation. For the past year Miss Coghlan has been in France, but her love for her native land has only become intensified by her absence from it, as will be seen in the poem written in France, which we place before our readers. Her lyrics have gained prizes from several English magazines. They are destined, we believe, to bring fame to their author of more than a temporary character.

MOONLIGHT ON THE WATER.

LIKE a pathway for the angels
    Falls the moonlight on the waves—
Lying in a silvery brightness
    O'er a hundred nameless graves.

Far across the ocean falling
    With its soft and gentle beam—
While the murmur of the waters
    Seems the music of a dream.

See! ten thousand starlight sparkles
    Gleam upon that pathway bright;
And I gaze till fairly dazzled
    By the glory there to-night,

For I almost think the angels
    Walk upon that glitt'ring sea,
Keeping watch above the sleepers
    Till they wake eternally.

And those shining ripples, falling
    Softly on the sandy shore,
Seem to whisper, "Peace for ever"
    When this restless life is o'er.

WAITING.*

I HAVE waited, waited, waited
    All the weary years and long,
While the summer flow'rs were blooming
    And the wild birds were in song;
'Mong the sunbeams pictures weaving
    Of the golden days in store,
Reading in the glowing blossoms
    Love's sweet message o'er and o'er—

* The above was awarded the prize offered for the best lyric in " The Muses."

" I am coming, darling, coming,
   Ere the blossoms droop to die ;
Some day, when the flush of evening
   Brightens o'er the western sky."

So I waited, waited, waited,
   Though the days were often long;
But the flow'rs – the flow'rs have faded,
   And the birds have ceased their song ;
While the sunbeams shine but dimly,
   Struggling through a mist of tears –
Vain ! O vain was all my waiting
   Through the light or gloom of years.
   " I am coming, darling, coming "–
     Still I hear the old refrain ;
   And I'm always waiting, waiting,
     Though he never comes again.

COMING !

HE is coming, coming, coming !
   O ! the sweetness of the word–
It is written on the flowers,
   'Tis the song of every bird.
After all the weary waiting,
   All the sorrow and the pain–
Just to think that I shall meet him,
   Meet my own true love again !
   " He is coming, he is coming"–
     I can hear it on the shore,
     Where the waves, once sadly sobbing,
     Murmur " coming" o'er and o'er.

" He is coming, coming, coming,"
   Breezes whisper all the day,
And the little sunbeams shine it
   As among the leaves they play.
O ! was ever known such gladness–

What a happy world is ours!
Shine still brighter, golden sunbeams,
Bloom yet fairer, lovely flowers!
    For he's coming, for he's coming,
        He will leave me never more—
    He is coming, coming, coming,
        And he loves me as of yore.

MY SOUL AND I.

I STOOP and kiss the blossoms,
    I breathe their fragrance in;
Against my face I press them—
    So pure from taint of sin.
And all I know of beauty,
    Of loveliness and light,
I'm wreathing close together
    In voiceless prayer to-night.

I look into the deepness
    Of yonder heaven's blue,
My soul within me burning
    To break its way right through;
But in that pain of longing
    I find no words to pray,
'Tis but the silent struggle
    Of spirit-life and clay.

Deep in my heart is echoed
    The song of every bird,
The murmur of the ocean,
    And every breeze that stirred
The little leaves that trembled
    Beneath the breath of day,
And yet my soul is panting
    For what it cannot say.

I gather up the sunbeams
That dance upon the stream;
I thread the glitt'ring dewdrops
Upon the pale moonbeam;
I weave the stars that twinkle
Upon the breast of night—
And yet my soul is longing
For something still more bright.

LINES WRITTEN AT ARCACHON (France).

ARCACHON! 'mong the pine trees tall,
Where none may count their number,
Where winds to gentler breezes fall,
And dreamy sunbeams slumber;

Where Peace itself has paused awhile,
With shining wings all furled,
And one may bask in Summer's smile
Oblivious of the world;

Or follow far the forest path,
So wild and wierd and lonely,
Where all companions that one hath
Are broom and heather only—

While pine trees whisper far above
Their wond'rous song or story
Of days of hate and days of love—
Of death, of life, of glory;

Or on the strand seek gleaming shells,
Frail trophies of the ocean,
Where sweetest music sinks and swells
With every ripp'ling motion.

But O, Arcachon! were each pine
Within thy forests growing
Made of the purest gold—more fine
Than light from sunbeams glowing;

And were thy shells all pearls, or filled
    Thy sands with treasures golden—
Yet never could my heart or will
    Be to thy land beholden.

For what art thou, O France, to me—
    What care I for thy treasure ?
My own dear land beyond the sea—
    I love *it* without measure !

Its woods, its fields, its light and shade,
    Its mountains, and its waters,
Are glories that can never fade
    For Erin's sons and daughters !

And proud I am to own thee mine,
    Though sadden'd is thy story—
Yet Erin we will not repine,
    But wait thy coming glory.

"NINETY IN SHADE."

(TO MABEL).

BY MR. HEBER COGHLAN.

" YOU think it is ninety degrees in the shade ?"
Yes ; that is the record I've mentally made.
But have you considered the magical cause
Of this innovation on natural laws ?

No ! Listen, dear Mabel—'Twas " zero" last week,
When much apprehension had blanched your fair cheek,
When Hope and her handmaid for ever seemed fled,
And fond aspirations were dying, or dead.

Some hovering spirit that still lingered near,
In sympathy, whispered a word in my ear—
" Despair not, but go to your Father and King,
And seek for *His* succour ; let sorrow take wing."

I felt disembodied, and sped from this Earth
With wings as if gifted with seraphim birth;
I glanced o'er the world and its satellite moon,
And Ocean lay dwarfed like a strip of lagoon!

I flashed past the planets, away beyond Mars,
And recked not of Saturn's eight moons and bars;
Away still I cleaved, through an infinite space,
Beyond telescopic and stellular race!

Away, still away! past all shadow and shade,
Till distance seemed lost in the progress I made!
The glory of Heaven gleamed fair in my view!—
And, Mabel, remember, *the plea was for you!*

The walls were of jasper, most dazzlingly bright;
The gate straight before me was a pearl of light—
It swung on a pivot of sapphire! Behold!
The streets of the city were gleaming in gold!

I paused not, but entered, and fearlessly went,
With soul quite elated, to where a bow bent
Above a white throne, which was partly concealed,
And, veiled in His majesty, *God was revealed!*

I poured my petition so fervently wild
I thought some minist'ring spirits there smiled.
A voice, scarcely audible—just "still and small"—
Then granted my prayer; yes, granted it all!

I uttered my gratitude, heartfelt and deep,
And then glided back 'long the fathomless steep,
Elated with transport and joy unexpressed
Because that *the sorrows of life were redressed.*

And then I concluded my future should be
A life of emphatic worth, Mabel, with thee;
And now do you doubt my thermometer made
At that time a record of "NINETY IN SHADE."

Charlotte Jobling.

———

THE names of some authors are prominently before the public as soon as—sometimes before—they have written anything worth reading. On the contrary, the works of some authors are better known than their names. Mrs. Jobling belongs to the latter class. Her works are frequently quoted by those who do not know her nationality nor perhaps her name. This arises from the fact that many of her contributions to Irish newspapers have appeared over a *non de plume*, about two hundred having appeared in the *Weekly Irish Times* alone, over the signature of "Irish Molly."

Mrs. Jobling is a native of Belfast, and at present resides in Dublin. She is a prolific writer; over eight hundred of her poems have already appeared in print. She has written over one hundred and fifty songs for music (old Irish airs) already in existence. There is scarcely any phase of life she has not depicted, and scarcely any style of versification she has not adopted. In 1893 she won the prize at the "Rondeau Competition" of "The Muses," an exceedingly difficult form of verse in which to excel. The sentiment of her poems is as diversified as the subjects. The gay, the grave, the humorous and the sentimental all come under her notice, and her powers of showing forth the varied emotional feelings of different characters in a single poem are unique. Some time ago a boat was capsized on Strangford Lough, and all its occupants, five in number, drowned. Mrs. Jobling thus describes a woman who, on hearing the news, came to the shore, whose husband and son had been in the ill-fated boat :—

> She stood upon the bleak sea shore,
> Her grey hair streaming wild,
> And aye she wept and wrung her hands,
> And called upon her child.
> " Why call ye but upon your boy ?
> Forget ye Andro' Nairne ?"
> " Him ! he's *another* woman's son—
> But man ! the bairn's *my* bairn ! "

Mrs. Jobling generally writes in the morning, sometimes before day-light. Her mode of composing is somewhat novel if not ingenious. She does not always commence at the beginning and end at the last verse. On the contrary she frequently composes the last verse first, then the first verse, filling up the middle according to her pre-conceived ideas on the subject.

Although an ardent patriot, Mrs. Jobling has a great disgust for party politics, and is of the opinion that Ireland's enemies do not all live outside our own green isle. Her poem " God save Ireland " breathes a spirit of the truest patriotism It is too long for insertion here, but we give a stanza as a specimen :—

> *May God save Ireland !* Many a thoughtless tongue
> Repeats the words in parrot-like rotation ;
> Poor, foolish Ireland that has been so long
> A grief and wonderment to every nation !
> God save her from herself, that worst of foes,
> God save her from her friends—so-called (ah, me !
> Such friendship culminates her direst woes) —
> And from all evil influence set her free !
> God save her ! never yet more needful prayer
> Arose from hearts to lips of Irishmen ;

Though clouds at times have lowered above her, ne'er
Cloud black as this has threatened her. But when
Man fails, then God is nearest; O may He
Be near us in this strait our voice to hear
In ceaseless supplication earnestly
Entreating —prayer to loyal hearts how near!—
May God save Ireland.

MOTHER'S SHIP.

"WHEN mother's ship comes in !"   "Ah me! how long we've waited –
The little ones and I—till she reach our barren shore ;
For all our mighty needs and our little pleasures freighted
With such absolute abundance that we'll wish for nothing more."

"When mother's ship comes in ! We'll have fires—such fires !—and
plenty
Of bread, and even butter –bread and butter—think of that !
We'll be warm and never hungry, never hungry—not for twenty—
Twenty years ! and there'll be milk, too, for dear old pussy cat.

'When mother's ship comes in !' There'll be books on board for
Harry,
There'll be frocks for Kate and Susie, and boots—pretty boots—
for me ;
And for baby such a dolly"   "O, my boys ! think ere you marry,
Nor leave your babes dependent on a mother's ship at sea !"

"' When mother's ship comes in !' It will bring us birds and flowers,
And for Will, who loves a doggie, there'll be one—nay, two or
three ;
And for mother, writing, writing, through tho long, long weary
hours"—
"If it bring your wishes, darlings, 'twill bring freight enough for
me.

'When mother's ship comes in !' So inured to disappointment,
Would I laugh or would I cry—could I bear success at last ?
O, the careless wounds inflicted ! Holds the future any ointment
Will obliterate the scars left by conflicts that are past ?

'When mother's ship comes in!' Where, where is it that she
    lingers,
She must surely be becalmed on some lone, lone distant sea.
Another disappointment!—sinking heart and trembling fingers;
    I ope—to find the dawning of assured success for me!

The sun has pierced the black clouds, and bright hopes burst into
    blossom;
Rushing forth to find the children—happy tear-drops falling fast—
I clasp them in my arms and I strain them to my bosom,
    Crying,'' Darlings! darlings! darlings! mother's ship's in port
    at last!' "

JACK'S WIVES.

THE love of my heart and I have been wed
    Seven years, just seven to-day.
And could we but forget Kilbride churchyard
    I might be happy and gay.
But he can't forget, and I can't forget
    And with grief my heart's aye swellin',
For he calls her his wife—his *wife*, while I
    Am never but Mary Ellen.

O, why did he marry me when he knew
    That he hadn't a heart to bestow?
For it clings to that grave in Kilbride churchyard
    Where Bessie is lying low,
With the babe on her breast, that breathed and died,
    And my woe is beyond all tellin',
For aye she's his wife—his *wife*, while I
    Am never but Mary Ellen.

Three bonnie lad bairns play at my knee,
    Two bright wee lasses beside;
But he gives to the two in Kilbride churchyard .
    More love than we all divide.
It's would, O! would that her place were mine,
    And that she at his side were dwellin',
For he calls her his wife—his *wife*, while I
    Am nothing but Mary Ellen.

THE ROSE OF PORTAVOGIE.

THE girl I love's an Irish girl,
  For Irish girls are rare ones;
There's not a place in all the worl'
  Can equal Ireland's fair ones.
An' not a foot of Irish groun'
  Her match could ever show me,
An' she lives in the County Down,
  The place is Portavogie.

Tho' I have travelled far and wide,
  Thro' many a foreign nation,
A girl like her I never spied
  In any situation;
For all the countries I've been in,
  There was not one to show me
A girl the match of Essie Quin,
  The Rose of Portavogie.

Here face is fair, an' very fair;
  Tho' tall she is, an' stately,
Her dancin' feet are light as air,
  Tho' fain to go sedately.
When near her every hour has wings
  (When far, but they go slowly!)
An' sweet-voiced as a linnet sings
  The Rose of Portavogie.

An' proud am I that Essie Quin,
  The girl I love so dearly—
The girl I'd give my life to win—
  Loves me as well—or nearly.
O, would the months but hasten on—
  They go for me too slowly—
Till I can make the girl I've won
  A Bride in Portavogie.

Thomas Given.

MR. THOMAS GIVEN, of Cullybackey, County Antrim, is well known in his native district as a poet of much real power and genuine feeling. He has not a little of the fire and pathos of Burns, and handles the Doric of the North in a way that would have delighted that great master of Scottish song. He owes little to his contemporaries or to the schools, but simply " sings because he must." In addition to a keen eye for Nature and a sympathetic insight into the motives and ways of men, he possesses the critical faculty in a high degree, and can cut at old abuses and present wrongs with a fearlessness and a thoroughness which are as delightful as they are effective. His poems, as they appear in the *Ballymena Observer* and other publications, are read with great interest. They deserve a better medium of preservation than that afforded by the ephemeral columns of a local newspaper.

TO A "BLUE BONNET."

WEE feckless mite o' Nature's wanes
Thy tiny strength e'en strength disdains,
Thy beauty disna gee thee pains
    To show or wear it,
Yet mighty man wae a' his brains
    Wull ne'er come near it.

Thine eye o' fire can sin detect
The snugly hid unseen insect ;
How quickly, tae, you can dissect
    What's tae your taste ;
But a' ye seem aye tae expect
    Some unknown haste.

Ye needna turn your head sae quick,
Nor lift your e'e at ilka pick,
Nae fear o' stane, or snare, or stick
        Need thee alerm;
What han' unboun' tae Keyless Nick
        Wad dae thee herm.

An' yet wae thee 'tis Nature's plan
To guard frae herm on every han':
Ye're no' your lane in this auld lan'
        O' show and screen,
Where treachery frae man tae man
        Is aften seen.

Abune yon bleak an' frozen bog,
E'er Simmer wrote its langest log,
I watched thee keek beneath the scrog
        In splendure dress't,
For leaves, or bits o' softest fog
        Tae big your nest.

But noo thy work is clean forgot;
Nae young yins cheep aroun' the spot
Whar yinst ye hid their cosy cot
        Frae school boys' e'e—
In a' a lesson you hae tought
        The likes o' me.

Tae be content within the sphere
That is tae us allotted here;
If ower oor pathways creep the breer
        Ingratitude,
Let's loup abune it wae a cheer
        As mankin' should.

MAY.

BRIGHT Queen of May, thy face is gay
  As the hopes of a youthful morning,
Where all is calm as the Sabbath psalm,
  Reflecting no shadow of turning.
No storm clouds gather to nip the flower
Which blooms in the garden of boyhood's hour.

Bright Queen of May, though you smile to-day,
  To some 'tis a smile of sadness,
Whose eyes are fled with their buried dead,
  'Mid sorrow akin to madness.
The hawthorn may flourish on many a stem,
And the lark praise his Maker unseen by them.

Bright Queen of May, in a bounteous way
  The daisies adorn thy path,
The violets shy with the bluebells vie
  To ensure you a perfume bath.
The fields make merry in Nature's plan,
And all is happy but thankless man.

Bright Queen of May, through the toilsome day,
  Man, weary and worn, must plod,
But his thoughts can spring on electric wing
  To the home of his Father, God;
And his heart may be cheered in the dreariest time
If his soul be sunned in the stream of rhyme.

Bright Queen of May, have you found a way
  Which pointeth to happiness here,
With slander flown and deceit unknown,
  And the future without a tear?
The Mayflower smiled in the warmth of noon,
Then answered sadly, go on till June.

Bright Queen of May, we have sought that way
  Through Nature's boundless scope;

Though her speech be fair as her song-girt air,
　No margin is found for hope.
No words to the weary and woe-begone
But the pitiless answer, go further on.

Frail mortal stay, quoth the Queen of May,
　And reason as mankind ought;
Why need you fret with a vain regret
　At the evils the fall hath brought ?
Will Calvary's sacrifice breathe no calm
In the future prepared by the great I Am ?

Reb. W. Cowan.

THE Rev. William Cowan belongs to a well-known
Galway family, and was born in the village of
Monivea, in that county, on the 31st August, 1833.
He was educated at the Irish Missionary College, Ballinasloe, with a view to the ministry of the Irish Church.
From an early age he was an enthusiast about poetry,
learning by heart long passages from his favourite authors –
Byron and Cowper—his later favourites being Tennyson,
Wordsworth, and Mathew Arnold. About the age of fifteen
he began to compose verse, and soon after, like many another
budding poet, sent his compositions to the local newspapers. He was a regular contributor to the *Loughrea
Journal* for some years, and published in it a series of
essays on various subjects, and a temperance story entitled
" Mervyn O'Connor: or the Broken Pledge;" and, when he
ceased connection with it, the editor wrote him " Willie,
we have Missed You," in allusion to the popular song of

that name, and requesting the continuance of his contributions. About this time Mr. Cowan wrote a long poem, after the style of Macaulay's " Lays of Ancient Rome," in celebration of Leonidas and his brave three hundred; but, to the author's mortification, the manuscript disappeared in some unaccountable way, and it never saw the light.

In 1863 Mr. Cowan married Emmy, eldest daughter of Thomas Fewster, Esq., Hull, Yorkshire, by whom he has had ten children, seven of whom are living. In 1870 he published a collection of his poems under the title of " Tourist Pictures, and other Poems." This work was well received by the public, and quickly bought up. As the author quaintly remarks, it gave him a twofold pleasure—first, that enjoyed in composing the poems; and, second, the profits realized by the sale of it induced Mrs. Cowan and himself to spend an extra holiday in visiting various places of interest in different parts of Ireland. In 1872 he took holy orders, and was licensed to the curacy of Gweedore, County Donegal, where he remained for three years, when he was appointed to the parish of Faughanvale, where he laboured for the next thirteen years. In 1878 he published a second volume, entitled " Poems: chiefly Sacred, including Translations from Ancient Latin Hymns." This work brought additional reputation to the author as a poet of very considerable ability and genuine power. In 1888 he was appointed incumbent of St. Augustine's, in the city of Londonderry, where he still resides. He is a regular contributor to *Leisure Hour, Good Words, The Quiver, Chambers' Journal,* and other magazines, and is at present engaged in preparing a volume of sermons for publication.

OLD VOICES.

ACROSS the seas they come to me,
　　Old voices of a happier day,
When love was young and hope was high,
　　And flowers grew bright about my way.
I sit within the rose-girt pane,
　　And watch the tranquil western sun
Dip gently in the golden sea,
　　And think of friends for ever gone,
And while I gaze and think, to me
There come old voices o'er the sea.

I hear them when alone I stroll
　　Along the white surf-beaten shore;
They mingle in the fisher's song
　　Heard 'mid the lull of ocean's roar;
And when with toilsome steps and slow,
　　I struggle up the fern-clad cliffs
Which slope in beauty from the bay,
　　And watch far off the fading skiffs,
They whisper of old times to me,
Those voices from across the sea.

So when night curtains sea and shore,
　　And white stars gleam across the wild,
And underneath the shadowy limes
　　With thoughts of other days beguiled
I linger long, too sad to rest,
　　For in this lonely heart of mine
There whisper as from long ago
　　Old echoes that have grown divine—
Old echoes from across the sea,
They whisper of old times to me.

A SUMMER DAY.

LET me lie here beneath this elm-tree old,
    And give myself, sun-shaded, up to thought—
    How beautiful the world! how blest my lot!
Behold around the cups of floral gold,
The scented hay, the green-robed whispering trees,
    Wild song birds piping in each leafy brake,
    Fair water-lilies carpeting yon lake,
The gorgeous dragon flies and murmuring bees!
How bright the clouds through which the vi'let sky
    Laughs at the emerald enamelled earth!
    And like a girl in her innocent mirth
The sun-flecked river, laughing, rushes by—
    Here would I gaze and dream and love and stay:
    Oh, slowly pass, thou lovely summer day!

'TWILL NOT BE ALWAYS WINTER.

'TWILL not be always winter, dear,
    There comes a brighter day,
And you and I shall by and by
    Fling gloom and grief away;
The icy streams will chant their bliss
    To rock and fern and tree,
And birds on high shall catch the joy,
    And sing to you and me.

And we shall feel the soft caress
    Of Summer's arms once more,
And wander where the buoyant air
    Shall bathe us o'er and o'er.
Ah, love, my love, take heart of grace,
    And know that late or soon
The frosts of Winter shall give place
    To the warm sun of June!

'Twill not be always winter, dear ;
  I see with faith's clear eye
A brighter time, a happier clime,
  A home beyond the sky.
Oh! there 'tis Summer all the year,
  God is Himself the sun—
Then hand in hand to that fair land
  Come, let us hasten on.

SPRING IS COMING.

SPRING is coming, Spring is coming,
    Let us run to meet her,
    Let us warmly greet her,
She is lovely, she is bright,
And the dawning year's grey light
Flushes all her handsome brow,
Let us run to greet her now.

Spring is coming, Spring is coming,
    Lightly see she trips,
    Let us kiss her lips,
And enfold her in our arms,
Radiant in her youthful charms ;
To her lovers all sweet things
In her fair white hands she brings.

Spring is coming, Spring is coming,
    In the vales and brooks,
    In the shady nooks,
On the mountains, in the meads,
Where the dewdrop's shining beads
Glorify the tender grass,
You may see her as you pass.

Spring is coming, Spring is coming,
    Strewing lovely flowers
    Down the rosy hours ;

See upon her radiant way
Crocus flames like eye of day,
Primroses around her rise,
Bluebells and anemonies.

Spring is coming, Spring is coming,
    Let us run to meet her,
    And with glad heart greet her;
She brings health in both her hands,
She gives beauty to the lands,
Calls the children forth to play,
Welcome, welcome, Spring and May.

Hamilton Drummond.

THERE are some occupations and professions which
are more favourable to the development of poetic
genius than others, and if we are to judge by the
numbers of poets who come to the front in the various
walks of life we will be inclined to conclude that the
occupation of the city merchant and manufacturer is less
favourable to the cultivation of literature than any other
in which educated men are engaged.   In Mr. Drummond
we have a notable exception to this general rule.   A busy
city merchant, a Justice of the Peace for the city of Dublin,
a member of several Boards of Directors of public
companies, honorary secretary of several societies,
and a genuine poet   In the midst of so much
matter of fact duties one wonders where Mr. Drummond
gets time to devote to the cultivation of the muse,—
especially as his writings show him to be well read in

classic literature, but "where ones inclinings lead to bardic flights make large allowance." The current of poetic fire which permeates the nature of the true born poet is not to be quenched even by the multitudinous duties of public life.

Mr. Drummond was born in the city of Dublin in the year 1857, and early in his career showed the possession of poetic ability. For a time his poems were published in various newspapers and magazines, and in 1882 he collected his first volume. "Sir Hildebrand, and other poems" was the title of it. Originality is a distinguishing feature of this work, and its pages are particularly free from the feeble re-echoes of other great minds with which first volumes are so frequently filled. It is the work of an original thinker. The poet's powers of observation, and close acquaintance with nature throughout it are everywhere visible, and these he has turned to good account.

In 1893, Mr. Drummond issued a second volume entitled "Herod, and other poems" (Kegan, Paul, Trubner & Co.) This work was favourably received by the press and the public, and increased the author's reputation as a poet of refined taste and keen poetic insight. The poem, " Herod," which gives the title to the book is a powerful monologue in blank verse, conceived with much dramatic skill, and grandly worded. The sonnets and lyrics are not less beautiful. They are full of choice thoughts and pretty fancies, and are delightful reading to lovers of Irish literature. Diversity of style, purity of diction, and elegance of expression, are distinguishing characteristics of the works of this highly gifted poet.

PISO'S SLAVE.

THE dogs of doom came baying,
And slavering in their breath,
With hungry lust for slaying,
And howling out for death—
        Death to Piso.

One met them, not a freed man;
Not even that—a slave;
But never while man need man,
Could man find man more brave
        Than he for Piso.

A robe of state cast round him,
He looked from Piso's place,
On those who came to hound him,
Their equal, in their face,
        For love of Piso.

Whom seek ye? Piso? Thrust, then,
Straight to the throat—thrust here;
Piso am I, and must then
Die, and know no fear;
        And lied for Piso.

More kingly he than Nero!
Tell it out while ages roll:
Bondsman with heart of hero,
A slave with a freeman's soul
        Who died—for Piso.

HUNGER.

MY soul was hungry, and one came and said,
  "Take these and eat;" and thrust into my hand
Dry husks of knowledge, and at his command
I fed and hungered, and still hungering, fed,
Nor found relief from hunger in the bread.

Another cried, " To him who would withstand
The aching pangs of nature, there is planned
Forgetfulness in labour."   But the dead
Alone have full forgetfulness ; my crave
Yearned bitterly upon me. is there naught
Can stay my hunger but the quiet grave,
Or bring the peace and comfort I have sought ?
Ah, love so far away, hast thou no touch
Of pity that I hunger overmuch ?

POWER.

OVER a crumbling arch of stone
That stands in a desert land alone,
The central arch of a city's gate,
Is written this truth from the book of fate—
    " Allah alone is great."

Nations are born and die away
Like a morning's mist at full noonday;
Empires that wield a mighty sway
And shake the world by their mighty power
Are but as the playthings of an hour.
    Allah alone is great.

Man with his busy, plotting brain
Planning and laying his life in train,
Born to a kingdom, or dowered with a crust,
Endures for a moment, then "dust to dust."
    Allah alone is great.

Worlds are created and pass to nought
As swift as flies a forgotten thought ;
Suns are darkened or turned to blood ;
Ocean obeys, and dries its flood ;
Valleys are stretched where the mountains stood,
    Allah alone is great.

I look in the heart of man and see
Stamped on its doors through eternity,
Graven in letters deep and broad,
Though blindness and pride may deny their God,
Though the present despair and the future fear
Be veiled from the eye by a sceptic sneer,
Still the heart of man and the eastern gate,
Both hear this truth from the book of fate—
      Allah alone is great.

SILENCE.

I HOLD that we are wrong to seek
    To put in words our deepest thought;
    The purest things by nature taught
Are turned to coarser when we speak.

That flower whose perfume charms the sense
    Grows hard and common to the touch;
    And love that's wordy overmuch
Is marred by its own eloquence.

For love, like sympathy, hath bands
    More strong in silence than in speech;
    And hearts speak loudest each to each
Through meeting lips and clasp of hands.

Nor could I hope for fitting word
    To form in speech the thoughts that start;
    The inner core of every heart
Hath yearnings that are never heard.

They are too subtle, and transcend
    The power of words to speak their right;
    We therefore shut them out of sight,
To burn in silence to the end.

For even as the Magi held
   Their fire as sacred, so I hold
   My love as holy, sacred-souled,
And pure as worshipped fire of eld.

Nor dare I stain with word or pen
   That inner purer love to thee,
   Whose higher nature raiseth me
Beyond the common line of men.

Rev. F. Langbridge, M.A.

THIS eminent author, although an Englishman by birth, is not only one of the best known writers in Ireland, but his foremost works have been produced since he settled in the land of his adoption; and, as the products of his pen are "racy of the soil," we think we can fairly claim him as an Irish writer. The Rev. Frederick Langbridge, M.A., was born at Birmingham, on 17th March, 1849. He received his education, first at the school of the Misses Rogers—sisters of Henry Rogers, author of "The Eclipse of Faith"—and afterwards at Edward the Sixth's Grammar School; subsequently he entered Oxford, and finally graduated M.A. at Merton.

Mr. Langbridge's taste for literature manifested itself at an unusually early period in life. At the age of five he had read some of Macaulay's works, could repeat nearly the whole of "Horatius ' by heart, and had composed his first poem—a long one. He can remember to this day the excitement in which he paced the study at home reciting the lines, but, as he could not write sufficiently well at

this period to commit it to paper, it has not been preserved. At the age of about thirteen his first published
poem appeared in the *Birmingham Gazette*. Shortly after
he sent some verses to *Good Words*, of which Dr. Donald
Macleod was editor. These were accepted, and from then
till now Mr. Langbridge has added many pleasing contributions to current literature. Iu 1876 Mr. Langbridge
took holy orders, and was licensed to the curacy of St.
George's, Kendal. Two years later he married—on being
appointed to the incumbency of Alla, a parish in a wild
and mountainous district of County Donegal. In 1879
he was appointed to St. John's, Limerick, of which he is
still the popular and esteemed incumbent. The following
are some of the volumes which Mr. Langbridge has issued
up till the present:—"Gaslight and Stars" (Marcus
Ward), "Sunshine and Song" (Eyre & Spottiswoode),
"Sent Back by the Angels" (Cassell), and "Poor Folk's
Lives" (Simpkins, Marshall & Co,). A large number of
the poems in these volumes consists of ballads and stories
in verse, a kind of composition in which Mr. Langbridge
excels. Indeed, as a writer of ballads and story-poems he
has few equals. He does not go far to seek subjects for
his muse; he finds them in his every-day surroundings.
His writings show him to be in deep sympathy with the
trials and difficulties of the poor. He is thoroughly
conversant with their habits of thought and mode of life,
and some of his descriptions of their struggles with
poverty and distress are extremely pathetic. He has also
a keen sense of humour, and in the hands of a skilful
elocutionist these story-poems are calculated to sway any
audience to laughter or to tears. Among the best of this
class may be mentioned "Sammy" and "Sent Back by the
Angels," but these are too long for insertion here. His

songs are very popular with musicians, and many of them
have been set to music by eminent composers. Mr. Langbridge is also the author of numerous prose works, and is
editor of the latest Christmas annual, "The Old Country,"
which has already established its claim to popular favour.

A TALE OF A TURKEY.

MY rooms are not of a princely pattern;
    The couch has springs which one can't but feel;
The girl that waits is a snub-nosed slattern;
    The knives are black, and the forks are steel.
A chum is welcome to roll and butter,
    A cup of tea or a glass of wine;
But I frankly own my surprise was utter
    When aunt declared she would come and dine:
It thrilled my heart with intense pulsations
    To learn that this excellent aunt of mine,
From whom I cherish my expectations,
    Was coming on Christmas Day to dine.

The air was raw, and the sky was murky;
    The feet slip-slopped on the slushy ground;
Yet I sallied forth and I bought a turkey,
    And sausages slung in a necklace round;
Of lemons a brace, and of sage a plateful;
    A bottle of port that was old and fine:
For what's expense to a nephew grateful
    Who's proudly expecting an aunt to dine?
It's freely acknowledged that ostentation
    Can never be reckoned a fault of mine,
But I know what's due to a dear relation
    Who's coming on Christmas Day to dine.

The day came round and the hour of dining;
    But frolicsome fiends were abroad that night
Filling the air with their shrieks and whining,
    Whirling the snowflakes in gusts of white.

Within, rare odours the sense were freighting,
    Not all of earth, and not all divine.
I called to Nancy, " It's useless waiting—
    Serve up the turkey and let me dine."
That bird, though high in my estimation,
    But seldom graces a board of mine.
To let it burn were a profanation,
    Though Queen and Court had been asked to dine.

I helped myself to some slices tender,
    Sausages crisp and not too fat.
Never did monarch, the Faith's defender,
    Banquet on royaller fare than that.
A wing came next, with a leg to follow,
    Washed down with blood of the purple vine ;
And I left in fine but a framework hollow,
    That scarce sufficed for a mouse to dine.
I viewed with satisfied contemplation
    The sculpture carved by that knife of mine ;
And I felt that life has its compensation,
    And come what will, it is sweet to dine.

I said my grace—and for once devoutly—
    I filled my glass, and I blew my cloud ;
But hark ! the knocker goes banging stoutly,
    A step comes up with a creaking loud.
I peered thro' the smoke—for the room was *quite* full—
    And saw benevolent gig-lamps shine.
" I'm late," said aunt, " for the night was frightful ;
    But here I am, and I *mean* to dine ! "
With nerves that fluttered with strange pulsations,
    I viewed that excellent aunt of mine ;
And I ceased expecting my expectations
    On hearing her say that she meant to dine.

COURTSHIP.

IT chanced, they say, upon a day,
    A furlong from the town,
That she was strolling up the way
    As he was strolling down—
She humming low, as might be so,
    A ditty sweet and small;
He whistling loud a tune, you know,
    That had no tune at all,
It happened so—precisely so—
As all their friends and neighbours know.

As I and you perhaps may do,
    They gazed upon the ground;
But when they'd gone a yard or two
    Of course they both looked round.
They both were pained, they both explained
    What caused their eyes to roam;
And nothing after that remained
    But he should see her home.
It happened so—precisely so—
As all their friends and neighbours know.

Next day to that 'twas common chat,
    Admitting no debate,
A bonnet close beside a hat
    Was sitting on a gate.
A month, not more, had hustled o'er,
    When braving nod and smile,
One blushing soul came through the door
    Where two went up the aisle.
It happened so—precisely so—
As all their friends and neighbours know.

James A. Glenn.

MR. JAMES ALEXANDER GLENN as a poet is distinguished for his genuine humour and sparkling wit. Born and brought up at Raphoe, a beautiful and fertile district in the County Donegal, about twelve miles from the city of Londonderry; his surroundings presented features of natural beauties that poet or painter might dwell on with delight and admiration. When at school, the youth seemed to have a decided taste for mathematics. When leaving school, about fifteen or sixteen years of age, he began to woo the muses, and frequently made parodies on some of the more popular poems of the great poets whose works he had been reading. These were generally of a humorous character, and have not been preserved.

In 1874 he entered the Inland Revenue Department of the Civil Service, but it was not until his appointment at Limavady, in 1881, that his writings began to appear in print, and his first published poems appeared in the *Coleraine Constitution* of that year. During the next two years he contributed a great many pieces to the same journal, as well as a novelette entitled "Died Heartbroken." The beautiful scenery in this neighbourhood stimulated the poet to pour forth its praises in song. His "Farewell to Roeside" was written when leaving this locality, in 1883, on his appointment to Strabane. Two years later he was again transferred to Londonderry. During these years he contributed many pieces to the *Derry Journal*, and several to the *Weekly Freeman*, besides prose sketches to *Chambers' Journal*. In 1888 he was appointed to

Belfast where he still remains, and many pleasing contributions from his pen are periodically to be seen in
several of the daily and weekly newspapers in that great
commercial city.

SWEET SIXTEEN.

SOME only prize the rose's bloom
　　When fully blown the flowers,
And think the day more fair at noon
　　Than in the morning hours.
But most I love the half-oped bud
　　When fringed about with green—
It minds me of the artless grace
　　Of bashful Sweet Sixteen.

The sultry noon's unclouded glare
　　Still lacks the charm of morn;
The flaunting rose's outspread leaves
　　Perchance conceal a thorn.
But 'neath the modest opening bud
　　No lurking thorn is seen,
Nor cunning arts e'er mar the grace
　　Of simple Sweet Sixteen.

The river as it nears the sea
　　May wear a statelier look
Than when, in sparkling, bounding glee,
　　It formed the mountain brook.
But 'neath its smooth unruffled flow
　　Are dangerous depths, I ween—
Just like the wiles of those dear maids
　　Who long have passed sixteen.

See Julia in her conquering hour,
　　The belle of fashion's ball —
Of courtly life the fairest flower,
　　Admired and praised by all.

Despite her calm triumphant glance,
    And proud majestic mien,
There lurks a sigh for simpler joys
    That pleased her at sixteen.

And though some think the rose more rare
    When fully blown the flower,
And say that noon is far more fair
    Than is the morning hour.
I still prefer the half-oped bud
    So neatly fringed with green,
That minds me of my own dear maid—
    Sweet rosebud of sixteen.

AN IDYL.

A MURMURING rivulet wound its way
    'Mongst meadows and woodlands fair,
Whilst the birds with many a merry lay
    Were thrilling the summer air.
The flowers on its banks bent down to kiss
    Its brow as it rolled along,
And its bosom sparkled in amorous glee
    As it murmured this old, old song—
Oh! a heart that's unloved is a wilderness,
    And life without love is vain,
But sweetly the moments go gliding past
    When we love and are loved again.

A nightingale sat on a hawthorn spray,
    'Midst the buds of the vernal year,
And softly warbled a tender lay
    To his mate, who sat listening near.
Then the melody burst over hill and dale,
    And the woods with the sweet notes rang,
Whilst all nature seemed hushed to hear his tale,
    And this was the song he sang—

Oh! a heart that's unloved is a wilderness,
    And life without love is rain,
But sweetly the moments go gliding past
    When we love and are loved again.

On a stile in the meadows a maiden sat
    And gazed on the summer scene,
Whilst Robin was humming a ditty near—
    And an amorous one, I ween ;
For she sighed and blushed, and then grew coy,
    As her ear caught the welcome strain,
And her bosom throbbed with a love-lit joy
    Responsive to this refrain—
Oh! a heart that's unloved is a wilderness,
    For life without love is rain,
But sweetly the moments go gliding past
    When we love and are loved again.

A SEA-SIDE SKETCH.

(A VAGUE STORY.)

THE even was fair, not a cloud in the sky,
The scene was the sea-side, the month was July—
July in its bright robes of soft summer light—
When a large silken parasol loomed on my sight.
It lay on the rocks, like a tent overblown,
Though some *hand* may have held it, I'm willing to own.
A gentleman's bamboo also lay nigh,
And a fat little poodle on all kept its eye.
Whilst to vary the scene, which monotonous grew,
A hand or an elbow would steal into view;
And sometimes a ringlet, tossed out by the wind,
Would tattle and say—" Something more *lies* behind"—
But what else was there can only be guessed,
That large silken parasol covered the rest.

I stroll near the spot—was it voices I heard ?
Oh, no ! it perchance was the scream of a bird.
Then a rustle of silk, whilst the parasol dips,
And anon came a sound like the touching of lips ;
Perhaps 'twas the " wild waves," but *someone* said low,
" Now Harry, how *can* you ?   Pray let my hand go—
Sure some one may see—there's a step, I declare !
Just look how you've tumbled and tossed all my hair"—
But how the thing happened can only be guessed,
A large silken parasol covered the rest.

And a few moments after some one gave a scream,
As a fussy old lady disturbed " love's young dream"—
" Oh, dear ! goodness gracious ! I say, Mary Jane—
Mr. Sparker here, too—we'll be late for the train."
And mamma and her charge rushed so quick from the spot
That the fat little poodle was almost forgot.
And as poor Mr. Sparker gazed after the pair,
He could only gasp out, " Well, by Jove ! I declare !"
Then he picked up his cane and stood up on the rocks,
And the next words he said were, " Confound the old fox"—
But what followed after can only be guessed,
The veil of obscurity covers the rest.

Wilhelmina E. Johnstone.

MISS W. E. JOHNSTONE is a native of the County Dublin, and is the only daughter of Mr. Eustace M. Johnstone, B.L., Dalkey.   She received her education for a time at home, and afterwards at the Alexandria College, Dublin.   At a very early age her taste for literature became apparent, and at fifteen she not only had read, but was familiar with a number of the great English poets, her favourites being Shelly, Keats, Poe, and Shakespeare.   Her mode of study was systematic.   Having read the works of one author her parents were in the habit of testing her knowledge of what she had gone over, marking out the imperfectly studied portions to be read over again.

Although not long out of her teens, this young poetess has written many beautiful poems, and a number of short stories.   Among other publications, her poems have appeared in "The Muses," "Poetry and Prose," and ' Weekly Irish Times."

WHITHER GOEST THOU ?

'TWAS in the dawn of morning,
      The skies were all aglow,
When Azaël's note of warning
      Summoned a soul to go—
Whither ? Ah! who knows whither ?
      Where mortal cannot see,
Where flowers cannot wither,
      Where all is purity,
And souls may dwell for ever
      In love's infinity.

RAIN.

I AM list'ning to the falling,
  To the falling of the rain,
List'ning to its constant splashing
In the gutters, and the dashing—
    To the dashing of the rain,
As it falls on trees and flowers,
In soft verdure-giving showers,
  Sweet refreshing drops of rain.

While the rain-drops shinning tremble
On the flowerets they resemble
  Jewels rare, with lustre bright,
  Diamonds glinting in the light
      Purest gems of crystal rain,
And a murmur soft but clear
Falls upon my list'ning ear,
  'Tis the trembling of the leaves,
  Leaves soft stirred by Summer's breeze,
  All a-dripping with the rain.

And while list'ning I am thinking,
Thinking what the rain can do,
  How the flowers its coming hail,
  And how sweet both hill and dale
      Blossom after Summer showers.
When all nature has been drinking
  Freshest draughts of Summer rain.

C. F. Alexander.

MRS. CECILIA FRANCES ALEXANDER is the daughter of Major John Humphreys, and was born in Dublin about the year 1830. In 1850 she was married to Rev. William Alexander, D.D., now Bishop of Derry, and himself an eminent poet. Of the literary career of this renowned poetess it is unnecessary to say much here, as it is so widely known. Many of her poems have found a place in works of standard literature, not only in this country, but throughout Great Britain and the colonies, and are more or less known in almost every land in which the English language is spoken. She is the author of at least half a dozen volumes of verse, issued at various dates from the year 1846, and it is worthy of notice that two of these were published while she was still in her teens.

Her poetry is distinguished by a sweet melodious flow, and the language is simple and effective. She is particularly happy in the art of writing hymns for children in which so few really excel. While adapting them to the simplicity and limited understanding of a child she is able to preserve the true poetic feeling, and to interpret the emotions of youth in language of great clearness and beauty.

THE BURIAL OF MOSES.

BY Nebo's lonely mountain,
  On this side Jordan's wave,
In a vale in the land of Moab
  There lies a lonely grave;

And no man dug the sepulchre,
  And no man saw it e'er,
For the angels of God upturned the sod
  And laid the dead man there.

That was the grandest funeral
  That ever passed on earth,
But no man heard the tramping
  Or saw the train go forth—
Noiselessly as the daylight
  Comes when the night is done,
And the crimson streak on ocean's cheek
  Grows into the great sun;

Noiselessly as the spring-time
  Her crown of verdure weaves,
And all the trees on all the hills
  Upon their thousand leaves:
So without sound of music,
  Or voice of them that wept,
Silently down from the mountain's crown
  The great procession swept.

Perchance the bald old eagle,
  On grey Bethpeor's height,
Out of his rocky eyrie
  Looked on the wondrous sight;
Perchance the lion, stalking,
  Still shuns that hallowed spot—
For beast and bird have seen and heard
  That which man knoweth not.

But when the warrior dieth
  His comrades in the war,
With arms reversed and muffled drum,
  Follow the funeral car.
They show the banners taken,
  They tell his battles won;
And after him lead his masterless steed,
  While peals the minute gun.

Amid the noblest of the land
    Men lay the sage to rest,
And give the bard an honour'd place,
    With costly marble drest,
In the great minster-transept,
    Where lights like glories fall,
And the choir sings and the organ rings
    Along th' emblazon'd wall.

This was the bravest warrior
    That ever buckled sword ;
This the most gifted poet
    That ever breathed a word ;
And never earth's philosopher
    Traced with his golden pen
On the deathless page truth half so sage
    As he wrote down for men.

And had he not high honour ?
    The hill-side for his pall,
To lie in state while angels wait
    With stars for tapers tall ;
And the dark rock-pines, like tossing plumes,
    Over his bier to wave,
And God's own hand, in that lonely land,
    To lay him in the grave.

In that deep grave without a name,
    Whence his uncoffined clay
Shall break again (most wondrous thought !)
    Before the judgment day ;
And stand with glory wrapped around,
    On the hills he never trod,
And speak of the strife that won our life
    With the Incarnate Son of God.

O, lonely tomb in Moab's land !
    O, dark Bethpeor's hill !

Speak to these curious hearts of ours!
And teach them to be still.
God hath His mysteries of grace,
Ways that we cannot tell:
He hides them deep like the secret sleep
Of him He loved so well.

Margaret Mortimer.

MISS MORTIMER is a native of the city of Wex-
ford. At the age of sixteen she entered Kildare
Place Training College, Dublin, with the object
of becoming a teacher. After two years of hard study in
this institution she received an appointment as principal
teacher of a school in the village of Clonlara, where she
has been teaching for the last four years.

Clonlara is considered by many the most beautiful
valley along the whole course of the Shannon. It is about
eight miles from the city of Limerick, and opposite the
famous Falls of Doonass, on the County Clare side. For
several miles on each side of the village the country is
studded with mansions and richly-wooded demesnes.
These, with the raging waters on the one side and the
Clare hills on the other, form a charming picture of scenic
loveliness. This is the district in which Miss Mortimer
first became known to the public as a poetess, and no
doubt her surroundings were favourable to the development of her poetic talent.

From a child she could compose verses, some of which
are still extant, and would do credit to a poetess of more

mature years.   Her first published poem was "The Wreck
of the Roumania," which appeared in the *Weekly Irish
Times* less than two years ago.   Since then she has become
a "Fellow" of the "Brotherhood of Poets" and several
lyrics of great depth and beauty from her pen have
appeared in *The Muses*, the organ of that society.   She is
at present preparing a volume for publication which she
hopes to issue in the course of a few months.   The
career of this young poetess, for so far, has been such as to
inspire us with bright hopes for a distinguished future.

SOME DAY.

"SOME day" I shall look for the last, last time,
On the radiant earth in the summer shine :
I shall watch the gleam of the dying day
As it wanes and merges in twilight grey ;
And I shall not know when its light is o'er,
That for me it may glisten never more.

"Some day" I shall stand in the old-time place
And look my last at each well-loved face :
And the dearest one of all to my heart
Perhaps will not know that so soon we part—
Will never dream that the loving breast
Must ere long lie down to its quiet rest.

"Some day" when I know not, the call may come,
And the Reaper gather the harvest home ;
And though all my heart doth yearn to stay,
When the Master beckons I must away—
Must lay down the love and unclasp the hands
That fain would hold me in mortal bands.

"Some day" when I pass from this world's dark night,
As I slip from the shadow into the light,

I shall see a gleam across Jordan's wave,
I shall grasp a hand stretched out to save.
And my soul through the river of Death's cold foam,
Shall reach at last its Heavenly home.

"Some day" when the grass grows over my head,
And the years on wings of wind have sped,
I shall pass from remembrance—yea, as though
I had never been : and I shall not know.
Oh, hearts that love me! be true alway
And think of me then as you do to-day.

———

"FAREWELL TO LOCHABER."

"FAREWELL to Lochaber," hear the pipes sounding,
O'er the long line of troops, every heart bounding,
Marching with heads erect, marching to glory,
Aye! and to sable shrouds spear-rent and gory.

"Farewell to Lochaber," theme not of gladness,
List to the cadence low brimful of sadness;
Many a heart was torn, home came to mind,
All that life held for them now left behind.

"Farewell to Lochaber," cease the sad strain.
Back from the purple hills, rolls the refrain ;
Farewell indeed for some—Oh! who can say
What fate the morrow brings ?   How ends the day ?

"Farewell to Lochaber," colours are flying,
Some men are blithe and gay, others are sighing.
Will they return again ?   Surely not all.
On the red battle-field many must fall.

"Farewell to Lochaber," Scotia's sons listen.
Stirs it your courage up ?   See their eyes glisten.
Fears all cast aside, pride gains the day.
Is it for men to weep ? weak women may.

" Farewell to Lochaber," battle is raging ;
Fierce is the struggle wild, brothers engaging ;
Forms that beat high with life now senseless clod ;
Red runs the tide of blood, well piled the sod.

Closes the day at last, black night comes on.
Oh, at what fearful cost battle is won!
See the great mounds of dead ! See how they lie !
Faces all cold and still, turned to the sky.

There lies the piper bold, rigid and stark,
Birds of prey hover round veiled by the dark ;
Winds of heaven lift his hair dabbled in gore ;
Shall he see home again ?   Ah, nevermore !

" Farewell to Lochaber."   Where are they all ?
Those that went forth in pride—say, did they fall ?
Only a few remain, shattered and worn,
Broken are lance and spear, banners are torn.

" Farewell to Lochaber " - tongues mute in death
Uttered it o'er and o'er, ere passed the breath
From the firm hearts and true, dying alone,
Far from the loved ones dear, country and home.

SUMMER DAYS.

THE summer sun is shining on valley, glade, and hill,
The golden light is gilding every tiny stream and rill ;
From fields of corn the lark has sprung into the blue above,
With pulsing throat out-swelling in a song of praise and love.

In cool green lanes all shadowed the flowers bloom and twine,
Fragrant woodbine, blushing roses, and the wild and clinging vine ;
The violets moist with dewdrops, and the pink-tipped pimpernel,
Adorn the mossy banks in every green and shady dell.

Cool zephyrs sweep and rustle, in music low and sweet,
Through leafy bending branches and fields of ripened wheat ;
The far-off hills in purple mists through all the livelong day
Seem reaching to the fleecy clouds that stretch so far away.

Soft scents and odours fill the air in sweetest incense flung,
While o'er the drowsy hamlet a golden haze is hung;
The gorgeous poppies, crimson-eyed, peep from among the trees,
And nod their prim and stately heads in every passing breeze.

Among the hay, with idle rakes, two lovers laughing stand,
And all the earth to them doth seem a fair enchanted land—
A land of sunshine and of flowers, where Love is lord and king,
Around whose feet dear buds of Hope and sweetest promise spring.

Two birdies sit and watch them in a swaying apple tree,
With saucy mien and glancing eyes, as bright as bright can be.
Amid the apple blossoms they sing their joyous lay
To the lovers 'neath the branches all through the long bright day.

O Summer time! O time of joy! Stay with us yet awhile,
We fain would clasp thee closer, we dread to lose thy smile.
Come with thy wealth of blossom, in all thy radiant gear,
Thou time of bloom and fullest life! thou queen of all the year.

Isa J. Gouk.

THE "gift of letters" was very early conferred on Miss Isabella J. Gouk, Cork. She says she can hardly remember a time when she could not rhyme. About the year 1884 she began to publish some of her "rhymes," and the editors of magazines as well as the reading public soon recognised what Miss Gouk herself was unable to discover, namely, that what she designated "rhymes" evinced poetical merit of a high order Her first poems were published in the *Christian Treasury*, and many pleasing contributions from her pen have since appeared in various magazines and newspapers. A fine moral tone and deep religious sentiment pervades all she writes.

ANGELS UNAWARES.

To a Friend on the Death of his Wife.

UNAWARES (while blinding sorrow
   Fain would see another near),
Angel visitants now hallow
   All she loved so truly here.

And it may be, as she left thee,
   In thy pain and grief and woe,
That they met her ere they found thee
   In thy loneliness below,

That she smiled as others bore her
   On their wings far, far away;
Breathed a blessing as they passed her
   Back to thee on that sad day.

For though He will ne'er forsake thee,
　　Though His angels ever keep
Watch below, methinks in mercy
　　Specials angels closely creep.

Nearest, when the heart is broken,
　　With the balm of Heaven above,
With the fittest word just spoken—
　　Whispered by the God of Love!

So, methinks they hover near thee
　　Veiled in snowy wings of light;
Visitants of love and glory
　　From her home so fair and bright.

EVERMORE.

HITHERTO my Lord has guided
　　All my pilgrim life, and now
When the tent once more is folded
　　Shall a care becloud my brow?

Memories of bygone changes
　　Now oppress this weary brain
As I hear dear trembling voices
　　Bidding me God-speed again.

And I fain would linger longer
　　As I clasp kind, faithful hands,
Were not Erin's shades far sweeter
　　Than the desert's burning sands!

Gain and loss both mark our progress,
　　Stars oft set behind the cloud;
But the same star ever guides us
　　Till the desert sands are ploughed.

Earthly hopes are ever fleeting—
Sunbeams wrought upon the sand ;
Angel footsteps when retreating
Traced by graves on every hand.

But the Smitten Rock still follows
Blessing all our pilgrim way,
Shielding us beneath its shadows
From the fierce o'erpowering ray.

Ever follows wheresoever
God Himself leads on before,
Till we cross the narrow river—
Till we reach the heavenly shore.

Till the sands of time have drifted
Into vast Eternity,
Till the light of God is lifted
On life's pain and mystery.

———

TEMPERANCE.

" Here goes in the name of God !"—" Life of Father Mathew."

Touch, oh, touch the harp of Erin,
Tune its long discordant strings,
Let its sweetest chords awaken
Memories of bygone things.

Politics and creeds may differ,
Temperance is common ground,
May strong hands uphold its banner,
Honoured all the world around.

Gentle woman loves its shadow
Resting on her peaceful home,
Blesses it upon the billow
Wheresoe'er her loved ones roam.

And she smiles and tells her children
Of " a bright and golden chain "
Which a noble son of Erin
Flung across life's troubled main.

Shews them that its links still glitter
Brightly as in days of yore,
Closely banding law and order,
Though his form is seen no more.

Ah ! she cannot, dare not linger,
For the tell-tale tear would start
O'er her anguish for a father,
Ere that chain had bound his heart.

But the happy wife and mother
Lifts her greatful heart to God,
Blessing Him for that reformer
Who now rests beneath the sod.

Rebecca Scott.

" DONEGAL POETESS."

MISS REBECCA SCOTT, Castlefin, County Donegal, is the youngest daughter of Mr. Joseph Scott, who owned a large weaving factory at Castlefin, and grand-daughter of Mr. William Scott, Londonderry, who first introduced the sewing industry into the North-west of Ireland about the year 1832. Her whole family con-nection have taken a deep interest in the development of the various industrial resources of that part of the country, and the poetess herself still spends many an hour with her pen for the furtherance of the same cause. At a very early age her taste for literature began to manifest itself, and since those juvenile days she has enriched Irish literature with many a gem of poetic excellence. She has already published two large volumes, in both of which the genius of the poet is distinctly traceable. Her muse is not limited to one style of versifying, nor to one class of subjects. She can be gay and cheerful, she can be sad and tearful. She has evidently studied human nature closely, for she describes the feelings and emotions with a vividness which makes us feel we are spectators of the incident about which she writes. Her *In Memoriam* pieces, by their exquisite pathos and delicacy are calculated to set in motion the tenderest chords of human feeling. She is also extremely happy in her treatment of the legendary pieces. They are beautifully conceived and narrated in a pleasing and fascinating style. Among the best of these are "Thelka, the Waif," "The Lady Clare," "The Bell of Atri," "The Scholar's Weapon," and "The Fate of a Water Lily." Her hymns and songs are quite as inspiriting. Their merit is not shaded by any of her other productions. Everything she has published is quite in keeping with the popularity which she enjoys as a writer. Her poetical works have given enjoyment and delight to a large circle of admirers, and many a testimony has been borne by gentlemen of culture and literary taste to the appreciation which her works have met with. She has often been congratulated by members of the Royal family on her productions, and in the year 1880 she was presented by the Government with a cheque for £200 from the National Bounty Fund in recognition of her genius, accompanied by a letter from Lord Beaconsfield, in which he said he was very pleased to be able to say that the merits of her poems

fully justified him in awarding her this acknowledgment.
Her works have also been thoroughly appreciated by the
public. The second volume which she issued, entitled
" Echoes from Tyrconnel," is, like its predecessor, now
out of print, and a third is eagerly expected.

THE FATE OF THE WATER LILY.

On the brow of a lake, in a mossy dell
Did a graceful water-lily dwell,
In lonely beauty without a peer,
For none of her kindred beside were near ;
And though far away from the haunts of men,
In the deep recess of that mountain glen,
Where human foot had but seldom moved,
No city belle was e'er more beloved.
The neighbouring wild flowers all confessed
That the snow which lay on the mountain's breast
Was not more spotless, pure, or fair
Than the gentle lily which flourished there.
The wild bird paused on his joyous wing
A tender lay in her praise to sing;
The broad-leaved fern made her soft green nest,
And the zephyr lulled her each eve to rest,
And a star looked down with a lover's eye
To guard her sleep oh ! so tenderly ;
And the truant bee who from hour to hour
Coquetted and toyed with each radiant flower
Folded his wings on her dazzling breast,
And hummed, " Sweet Lily, I love thee best ;"
And so happy was she in that peaceful spot
That she never once wished to change her lot,
Till a babbling stream, as he danced along,
Assailed her ears with his gay love song.
" Oh ! peerless flower with the golden crest,
Fair as the snow on the mountain's breast,
Oh ! why dost thou waste in this desert place

Those charms which a royal court might grace ?
Oh ! come with me and my arms shall bear
My radiant queen to a home more fair
Than you ever saw in your brightest dreams,
Where sparkling fountains and laughing streams
Lave velvet banks ; where thy kindred fair
In myriads gleam in the gay parterre ;
Where the tulip rich with a thousand dyes
Unfolds her robes to the gorgeous skies,
And the clambering vine with its broad cool leaves
Round the trellis its graceful tendrils weaves ;
Where the jasmine white and sweet eglantine
Round fair ladies' bowers in rich clusters twine,
And the beds are bright with the aster's bloom,
And the heliotrope mingles its rich perfume
With the purple violet's balmy breath
And the odours borne from the thymy heath ;
Where the blushing rose, as yet, is queen,
Though soon shall the sceptre pass, I ween,
·From her grasp when her slaves thy charms shall see,
For what is the rose when compared with thee ?
Her perfumed breath is sweet, 'tis true,
And her crimsoned petals fair to view,
But 'neath her velvet-like mantle worn
She hides full many a cruel thorn,
As those who succumb to her fatal spell
By bought experience too oft can tell.
Then who would compare her blushing face
With my queenly lily's stately grace ?
Or her thorn-protected flaunting dress
With my darling's robe of gentleness ?
Then come, oh come, I have loved you long—
Nay, bend thine ear to my raptured song,
Of all thy suitors I love thee best ;
O, glance but once in my limpid breast,
And say if thou seest not reflected there
Thy golden crest and thy form so fair."

And day by day as he danced along
He poured in her ears his impassioned song,
Till the lily mistaking *mere sound* for *sense*,
And bewildered quite by his eloquence,
Found her bosom swell with a new-born pride,
And turned from her early friends aside;
From the simple strains of the forest birds
To hang with delight on his high-flown words;
From the loving stars' soft silvery beam
To the bubbles which danced on the laughing stream;
And the bee who still on her breast reposed,
To his tender hum found her ears more closed;
And one morn she was missed from her ferny nest,
And the streamlet had borne her away on his breast.

Who so happy as she as they danced along
To the merry chime of his ceaseless song?
Past a meadow now, then a stately wood,
In whose shade some lordly mansion stood;
While the birds who dwell in those grand old trees
Filled the air with a thousand melodies!
Or some tiny cot round whose low-browed door
Played forms she had never seen before,
Fair, spotless childhood, with brows as fair
As her own pure breast, and whose rippling hair
In the sunlight shone, like her golden crest
Which gleamed so bright on the streamlet's breast.
And still they danced gaily on, till she
Unused to such boisterous gaiety
Grew dizzy and faint and ceased to smile,
And sighed, " Dear Stream let us rest awhile
Or my feeble strength will soon be gone;"
But he laughed at her fears and went dancing on,
And the radiant visions passed away,
And at noon the course of the streamlet lay
O'er yawning chasm and sharp edged-rocks,
And the lily's breast from their cruel shocks
Was wounded and stained, and the fierce red sun

Beat down as he never before had done
On her now unsheltered and drooping head,
And she sighed in vain for her ferny bed;
And she saw and the sight made her pallid with fear
That the stream impatient her plaints to hear,
No longer bore on his stormy face
The smiling ripples which lent such grace
To his open brow, but an angry foam
Rose to his lips when she spoke of home;
And soon as the day passed slowly on
She saw that his short-lived love was gone;
And evening found her weary and worn
With spirits broken and petals torn,
Bewailing in sadness her hapless lot,
And at last when they reached a calm sweet spot
Where a lovely wild flower stooped on the brink
Her graceful head from the stream to drink,
She heard him chant in the self-same words
The strain that had thrilled to her own hearts chords,
In the blushing beauty's delighted ears,
And turned away to conceal her tears,
And meekly bowing her aching head
In a voice half choked with sobs she said—
" Oh! fickle streamlet why did you come
To tempt me away from my peaceful home ?
How happy there I might now have been
If thy treacherous face I never had seen,
But too late I mourn the die is cast,
No power on earth can retrieve the past,
Yet see far beyond yon line of fome
Lies a tiny lake which resembles home.
Oh! would I could manage to reach its bank,
And nestling down 'mid those ferns so rank,
There hide my wrongs and my misery
And lay me down in peace to die "
Then the streamlet tired of her long address,
More tired of her faded loveliness;

And of those reproaches which he knew
From the injured lily were justly due,
Bore her aside to the shady bank
And laid her down 'mong the fern leaves rank,
And then in reply to her farewell moan
Laughed a mocking laugh and went dancing on
To woo some other flower as fair,
And leave her when won to the same despair.

And the hapless lily, deceived and lone,
Breathed out her life in that farewell moan ;
And the forest birds her requiem sung,
And a shroud of moss o'er her pale corse flung ;
And the gentle star who had traced her flight
Shone still o'er that spot on the darkest night,
And looked sadly down with a lover's eye
To gard her grave, oh ! so tenderly.
Methinks my tale can no morel need,
It is so plain: " They who ruu may read."
The simple songs of the forest birds
Are truer by far than high-flown words ;
And the quiet love of a steady star,
Than impassioned vows, more enduring far ;
And the lily who lists to a flattering tongue
May, like the flower whose fate I have sung,
Have deep and heartful cause to rue
That she ever changed tried friends for new.
But alas ! the lesson may learn to late
To avoid the poor water lily's fate.

HARP OF MY OWN DEAR LAND.

HARP of my own dear land ! fain would I take thee
　　Down from the willows where thou hangest long,
From Sorrow's sad, inglorious sleep to wake thee
　　Into the full, deep tide of rapturous song.

With Hope's fair flowers thy golden strings entwining
  Strike deathless strains from out thy matchless chords—
Triumphant chords, like one of old combining
  Heroic measures set to deathless words.

Harp of my own dear land! in vain my longing;
  My woman's hand, alas! is all too weak—
Too sad the mournful memories that come thronging,
  Too fresh the tears on Erin's pallid cheek.

The eyes that love thee best are dimmed and tearful,
  Their dew falls heavy on thy trembling strings ;
And brooding o'er thee fierce, and grim, and fearful,
  Dark Discord sits, with gaunt, unlovely wings.

And though, beloved harp, around thee lingers,
  Like faint, sweet echoes of a happier time,
The thrilling touch of magic, minstrel fingers—
  Harmonious melodies of bards sublime.

So long thy notes have been attuned to sadness,
  Such plaintive pathos mingling with the strain,
That when thou fain would'st burst in songs of gladness
  Sad minor chords steal through the sweet refrain.

Harp of my own dear land ! how unavailing
  My feeble touch to break the spell of years,
While thorns around thy faded wreaths are trailing,
  And cold mists gather on thy strings like tears.

Some minstrel hand in happier days may take thee
  Down from the willows where thou slumb'rest long,
From Sorrow's sad, inglorious sleep to wake thee
  Into the full, deep tide of rapturous song.

W. T. M'Carthy.

MR. WILLIAM THOMAS M'CARTHY is the youngest son of Mr. George M'Carthy, and was born at Midleton, County Cork, on 8th December, 1864. He attended the Christian Brothers' school until about the age of eleven, when he removed to Carrigtwohill, where his elder and only brother was teacher of the local national school. Here he made rapid progress, and at the Intermediate Examination in 1880 obtained a creditable place in the Junior Grade, and had similar success in the Middle Grade the following year. In 1883 his brother died, and the lad returned home to Midleton. He now determined to try the Civil Service, and with this object he passed the preliminary examination for Second Class Clerkship. In the meantime he was offered a situation as solicitor's clerk, which he accepted. This position he retained for over four years. In 1888 he became connected with the Press as Midleton correspondent of the *Cork Daily Herald*, and subsequently extended his connection to the *Freeman* and other Dublin and English newspapers and news-agencies. During the time he was in the solicitor's office he learned shorthand, which was now of great service to him. In 1892 he removed to Queenstown, where he followed his journalistic pursuits, frequently contributing poems and sketches to the Cork and Dublin newspapers. Lately he has taken up his abode in the city of Cork, and the fruits of his prolific pen appear from time to time in the *Cork Weekly Herald*, *Weekly Irish Times*, and other publications.

YOUNG HEARTS' LOVE.

IS love not like a crystal stream
   That never can run dry ?
Is love not like a fair, fair dream
   That comes we know not why ?
Oh ! love is gay in youthful days,
   When life is fresh and sweet,
When Cupid slays in wily ways
   With darts all swift and fleet.
      As fair as e'en the fairest dream
        Is love in youthful days,
      As sparkling as a crystal stream
        Illumed by Sol's bright rays.

My love for thee is like a stream
   That flows so strong and clear ;
From out my heart wherein doth beam
   Love's light for you, my dear ;
And as a dream love came to me
   To be by Time ne'er chilled ;
My heart for thee shall ever be
   With love, with true love, filled.
      As fair as e'en the fairest dream
        Is love in youthful days,
      As sparkling as a crystal stream
        Illumed by Sol's bright rays.

THE EXILE'S REQUEST.

TAKE me back, take me back, to old Ireland again,
   Take me home to the " Isle of the West"—
To the land of my sires that I yearn to see,
   To my own native spot there to rest.
It is years, many years, since I parted from home,
   It is long since I left Erin's shore,
And now I'm grown old and my heart's one desire
   Is to see the old country once more.

Take me home, then, to Ireland, far over the sea,
    Take me back to green Erin so fair,
E'er the fast closing years of my life be all run,
    In sweet peace to end my days there.
Let me live once again in my dear native land,
    In the place where my forefathers dwelt,
And feel o'er again those emotions of joy
    That in boyhood I oftentimes felt.

To the green fields of Erin, beloved Innisfail,
    Take me home to that isle far away—
To the time when I'll see dear old Ireland again,
    Oh, my heart, how it longs for the day!
Take me back to the hills and the dales all so dear,
    Where often I roamed when a boy,
And many an hour in my youth there I spent—
    The thoughts of those days give me joy.

Take me home to the land that I oft see in dreams,
    To the fair land of Erin so green,
Where the sun shines so bright, where the birds sing so sweet,
    And kindly hearts gladden each scene.
Take me home to old Ireland, the land of my birth,
    From whence I've been long forced to roam—
To the land of my youth, to me dearest on earth,
    To the Emerald Isle take me home.

THE SONG OF THE BIRD.

ONE evening bright in early Spring,
    Ere yet the sun had gone to rest,
I heard a little, wild bird sing
    In notes so clear—it sang its best
Perched on a tree, as I stood near,
    High overhead on bough above,
A song so beautiful to hear
    It seemed a plaintive song of love.
'Twas the charming song of that bird on the tree
That evening in Spring had enraptured me.

All through the air the soft notes rang—
  Where silence dull had reigned before—
In song as sweet as e'er bird sang,
  I listened on 'til all was o'er ;
This little bird sang wild and free
  A song so grand, perched there on high,
Amidst the branches of the tree,
  It sang calm evening's lullaby.
'Twas the charming song of that bird on the tree
That evening in Spring had enraptured me.

𝖂. 𝕭. 𝖄eats.

R. WILLIAM BUTLER YEATS is the son of
an eminent artist, and was born at Sandy-
mount, a suburb of Dublin, in the year 1866.
The years of his childhood were spent mostly in Sligo,
the country to which his mother's people belong. The
fine bracing air, the free-and-easy manners of the people,
and the folk-lore so abundant in this part of the country,
all exerted an influence whose effects are now to be seen
in the popular author of so many entertaining books.
About the tenth year of his age he removed to London,
where for the next few years he attended the
Godolphin School, Hammersmith. Four years later his
father returned to Dublin, and the youth was sent to the
High School, Harcourt Street. After completing his
school education here, he became an art student, but soon
forsook art and adopted literature as a profession. The
first attempt he made at serious poetry, he tells us, was

when he was about seventeen, and much under the influence of Shelly. It was a dramatic poem, and was written in rivalry with a schoolfellow. His next was "Time and the Witch Vivian," which is included in the first volume of his poetical works, "The Wanderings of Oisin," published in 1889. A few years ago Mr. Yeats' father and family took up their residence in London, and in that active centre of the literary world scarcely a year goes by without some new work appearing from the busy pen of this young poet. In 1892 Mr. Yeats published a second collection of his poems under the title of "The Countess Kathleen" (T. Fisher Unwin). This work consists of two parts—the first a dramatic poem, from which the book obtains its title, and which the author says "is an attempt to mingle personal thought and feeling with the belief of Christian Ireland." The remainder consists of legends and lyrics, all rich in mellow harmonies and graphically-drawn pictures of Irish scenery, or incidents in Irish life. This work was well received, and not only sustained, but increased, the reputation which Mr. Yeats' earlier work had secured him as a poet of lofty thought, and fine descriptive talent. Poetry is not the only department of literature in which Mr. Yeats has made a name for himself He is more widely known as a writer of fairy tales. Of these he has published several volumes, which have had a wide circulation. His object in writing these will be seen in the following quotation from his latest work, "The Celtic Twilight, a Book about Men and Women, Dhouls and Fairies." In it he says, "Next to the desire which every artist feels to create for himself a little world out of the beautiful, pleasant, and significant things of this marred and clumsy universe, I have desired to show in a vision something of the face of Ireland to any of my own people who care for things of this kind. I have, therefore, written down accurately and candidly much that I have heard and seen, and except by way of comment, nothing I have merely imagined."

Mr. Yeats is at present preparing another volume of poems for publication. In the words of Mrs. Hinkson, he is "full of literary activity and plans, many of which are sure to be fulfilled, for with all his dreamy temperament he has a gift of energy and perseverance. There is not one of the younger men to whose career one looks with keener hope and faith."

THE LAKE ISLE OF INNISFREE.

I WILL arise and go now, and go to Innisfree,
    And a small cabin build there, of clay and wattles made ;
Nine bean rows will I have there, a hive for the honey bee,
    And live alone in the bee-loud glade.

And I shall have some peace there, for peace comes dropping slow,
    Dropping from the veils of the morning to where the cricket sings
There midnight's all a glimmer, and noon a purple glow,
    And evening full of the linnet's wings.

I will arise and go now, for always night and day
    I hear lake water lapping with low sounds by the shore ;
While I stand on the roadway or on the pavement grey,
    I hear it in the deep heart's core.

FATHER GILLIGAN.

THE old priest, Peter Gilligan,
    Was weary night and day,
For half his flocks were in their beds
    Or under green sod lay.

Once while he nodded on a chair,
    At the moth-hour of eve,
Another poor man sent for him,
    And he began to grieve.

"I have no rest, nor joy, nor peace,
    For people die, and die;"
And often cried he "God forgive!
    My body spake, not I,"

And then, half-lying on the chair,
    He knelt, prayed, fell asleep;
And the moth-hour went from the fields,
    And stars began to peep.

"And is the poor man dead?" he cried.
    "He died an hour ago."
The old priest, Peter Gilligan,
    In grief swayed to and fro.

"When you were gone he turned and died
    As merry as a bird."
The old priest, Peter Gilligan,
    He knelt him at that word.

"He who hath made the night of stars
    For souls who tire and bleed
Sent one of his great angels down
    To help me in my need.

"He who is wrapped in purple robes,
    With planets in His care,
Had pity on the least of things
    Asleep upon the chair."

They slowly into millions grew,
    And leaves shook in the wind;
And God covered the world with shade,
    And whispered to mankind.

Upon the time of sparrow chirp,
  When the moths came once more,
The old priest, Peter Gilligan,
  Stood upright on the floor.

"Mavrone, Mavrone! the man has died
  While I slept on the chair;"
He roused his horse out of its sleep,
  And rode with little care.

He rode now as he never rode,
  By rocky lane and fen;
The sick man's wife opened the door:
  "Father! you come again!"

————※————

John Kee.

————

DONEMANA, the birth-place of Mr. John Kee, is situated in Co. Tyrone, about six miles from the town of Strabane. Mr. Kee's father was a farmer, and until manhood the poet was employed on the farm. The cultivation of the muse, however, was not left out of sight. When at the plough he would work out his subject, and after nightfall, during the long winter evenings he would commit it to paper. In this way his ability to compose verse of very considerable ability soon made itself apparent. These effusions were mostly sent to the local newspapers, whose editors encouraged him by inserting them. His love of books increased as time wore on, and this is probably what induced him, after getting married, to adopt a business which would afford him better facilities for more extensive reading, and so he removed to Ballymena, and started business as a bookseller. Here he got acquainted with David Herbison, "Bard of Dunclug," and James Watt, two poets of more than local fame. After staying about three years in Ballymena he gave up business, and took a situation in the city of Limerick. The splendid scenery in the neighbourhood became the subject of his pen, and the poems he composed at this period still rank among the best of his productions. After about three years' stay in Limerick his brother died, and he returned again to the old homestead, where (with the exception of a short time in Coleraine) he resided for the last eighteen years. In addition to farming he has been doing a little at the printing business. He printed several small collections of his own works. His taste for printing has so far developed itself that within the last few months he has parted with his farm and gone to the town of Donegal to follow the business of a printer. In the course of his career Mr. Kee has published a great deal of poetry, and the gift of the genuine interpreter of nature is visible in every poem. His descriptions are singularly fresh, and many of his poems have a local significance which will make them ever prized in the locality which gave inspiration to them. Up till the present he has issued the following works :—"The Voice of the Heart," "Idyls of Youth," "The Ruins of Love," "Spray," and "Snow Wreaths." It is not too much to expect additions from time to time to this list of readable little volumes.

THE FALLS OF DOONASS.

WHEN the summer and the winter
  On the field of distant years,
With long burnished shafts of sunshine,
  And with gleaming icy spears,
Were contending at the birthtime
  Of the merry-hearted Spring,
Came a day when to the flowers
  All the rainbow colours cling.
When the skies and groves were mirrored
  On a flood of liquid glass,
And the woodland warblings echoed
  From Mount Shannon to Doonass.
O, Doonass of rushing rapids!
  Bound with wood and rocky steep,
Girt with modern hall and mansion,
  Crowned with ancient tower and keep;
O, Doonass, for beauty peerless,
  For wild grandeur all sublime!
The romance of the romantic
  Of our own wild lovely clime!

By the ivy-mantled turrets,
  Guarding still the grand old wood,
Sat the lovely Mary Massey
  Gazing sadly o'er the flood;
Not the madly running torrent,
  Not the rapture of the spot,
Stirred her bosom like a billow,
  By the inner tides of thought.
Her's the warmer, deeper passion
  Of a love that filled each sense,
Which a recent lover's quarrel
  Made more burning and intense;
For from earliest days of childhood
  Had a love, like summer air,
Or their own sweet southern sunshine,
  Circled Mary and Lord Clare.

But last eve a breath, a whisper,
  Such as haunts love's lucid strand,
Rose a tempest, wild and sudden,
  And they parted cold and grand.
Could such parting be for ever?
  Could it quench the love of years?
" Oh, it may, it may," she murmured,
  And still faster fell her tears.
And she cried—" His ship at Limerick
  Waits the tide of early morn,
For a far and stormy ocean—
  Oh! he never may return!
Yet to-night his farewell meeting
  Shall replace him by my side.
No, we must not part in anger!
  Love must triumph over pride."

Gently fell the tranquil twilight
  Round the gentle-hearted maid;
Stealing slowly up the river
  Crept the white mist's snowy braid;
Crept upward till the tree-tops
  Of Mount Shannon stood alone,
Towering o'er the fleecy billows,
  Rolling up and rolling on.
" Hasten hither," cried fair Mary,
  " Trusty boatman, launch your cot;
Pull me over, for the darkness
  Settles thick on every spot."
" Gentle lady, wait for moonrise:
  See the fog crawls dense and white;
Hear the Falls above and under—
  There is danger here to-night."

" Timid, are you, as a maiden,
  With your boat, the " Shannon's Pride?"
Have not I, a girl, oft paddled
  To the Castleconnell side?"

" Blame me not, my noble lady,
   Not to-night you cross alone;
Well I know my native river,
   Every current, every stone.
Bravest boats that shoot these rapids
   In my wake have quailed with fear ;
Yet for your sweet sake, fair lady,
   I would tarry now and here."
" For my sake, then, do not linger -
   O, I cannot, cannot stay !"
And her voice was choked with sobbing,
   And her tears gushed forth like spray.

" Take your seat—now firm and steady !
   With the help of God we'll pass ;"
So the boat shot like an arrow
   To the rapids of Doonass.
And through night and roaring waters
   Rung the paddle's measured lave,
Beating faster as it blended
   With the rushing of the wave.
O, that swift, deceitful current !
   O, the pall of mist hung there !
There is woe for that frail vessel—
   There is woe for young Lord Clare !
Wildly watching by the river,
   With the rapture and the pain
Of a love, the best and brightest
   Shining freshly after rain.

Faster beat the nearing paddle,
   Darker still the misty pall ;
" Steer for me," the lover shouted—
   " You are running on the Fall."
Still the boatman's stroke came quicker,
   But his rigid lips were dumb ;
Yet a girl-voice skimmed the water,
   Clear and sweet it said " I come."

But next moment   all was silent,
   Then a wild and grating crash,
With a shriek that rose terrific,
   High above the torrent's dash.
Long and far that death-cry sounded
   In the heart of gorge and glen ;
But through lifelong years the echo
   Wrung his heart who heard it then.

Rose next morning's sun as brightly,
   Smiled as beautiful the scene,
Sang as sweet the summer song-birds,
   As if nought of grief had been.
But sweet Mary and the boatman,
   The beautiful—the brave,
To the gladness and the sorrow,
   Were asleep beneath the wave.

Aubrey de Vere.

FOR upwards of half a century the subject of this notice has occupied a foremost place among the *litterateurs* of his native land.   Both in prose and poetry he has shown himself to be possessed of the literary gift in a high degree, and in the collected works of several of the Irish bards of the present day we find a song in praise of his writings. Mr. Aubrey de Vere was born at Curragh Chase, Co. Limerick, on 13th January, 1814. He is the third son of Sir Aubrey de Vere who was a poet of note, and is brother of Sir Stephen de Vere, also a celebrated poet and miscellaneous writer. He was the intimate friend of the late Lord Tennyson, and was well acquainted with Wordsworth and others of the "great masters" who have recently passed away, as well as many who are still in the front ranks of English literature, whose busy pens and fertile brains from time to time furnish us with so much intellectual enjoyment.

The published works of this eminent poet are so numerous and varied that they form a small library in themselves. Prominent among his poetical works may be mentioned—"The Waldenses or the Fall of Rora, a lyrical tale, with other poems," 1842. "The Search after the Prosperine and other poems, Classical and Meditative," 1843. "Innisfail and other poems, a lyrical Chronicle of Ireland," 1862. "The Infant Bridal and other poems," 1864. "Alexander the Great, St. Thomas of Canterbury and other poems," 1867. "The Legends of St. Patrick, and Legends of Ireland's Heroic Age,' 1872. "May Carrols." 1881. "Legends of the Saxon Saints," "The Foray of Queen Meave," and "Legends and Records of the Church and the Empire." In 1893, his latest works, "Mediæval Records and Sonnets" (Macmillan & Co.) was published. The specimens we give are taken from this volume. He is also the author of numerous prose works, the most notable of which are "Picturesque Sketches of Greece and Turkey," and "Hibernia Pacata."

"IS LIFE WORTH LIVING?"

LIFE is a thing worth living to the brave
Who fear not Fortune's spite, in Truth who trust,
Whose spirit, not thralled by pride or earthward lust,
Stands up while mortal tumults round them rave
Like Teneriffe above the ocean wave;

Who, mailed in Duty, with divine disgust
Recoil from frivolous joys and aims unjust,
Nor miss rewards which reason scorns to crave.
Life is worth living to those souls of light
Who live for others and by gift bestow
On them the jubilant beams, their own by right;
Who, knowing life's defects, more inly know
This life is not the Temple but the Gate
Where men, secure of entrance, watch and wait.

ROBERT BRUCE'S HEART; OR, THE LAST OF THE CRUSADERS.

" THIS tediousness in death is irksome, lords,
To standers-by : I pray you to be seated :"
Thus spake King Robert, dying in his chair.
His nobles and his knights around him stood
Silent, with brows bent forward. He continued :
" Because ye have been loyal, knights and peers,
I bade you hither, first to say farewell;
Next, to commend to you a loyalty
Not less, but greater, to your country due,
For I to her was loyal from the first.
She lies sore shaken; guard her as a mother
Her cradled babe, a man in strength his sire.
Guard her from foreign foes, from traitors near,
Yea from herself if evil dreams assail her.
Sustain her faith; in virtue bid her walk
Before her God, a nation clad with light."
He spake; then sat awhile with eyes close shut.
At last they opened; rested full on one
The sole who knelt : large tears—he knew it not—
Rolled down his face : 'twas Douglas. Thus the king :
" That hour we spake of oft, yet never feared,
O best and bravest of my friends, is come.
James, we were friends since boyhood; side by side
We stood, that hour when I was crowned, at Scone—

Crowned by a woman's hand when kinsmen none
Of hers approached me. Many a time we two
Flung back King Edward's powers. Betrayed, deserted,
By bloodhounds tracked we roamed the midnight moors;
I saw thy blood-drops stain Loch Etive's rocks;
Thy knees sustained my head, when faint with wounds,
Three days on Rackrin's island-shores I lay.
One night—rememberest thou that night?—I cried,—
Randolph, I think, stood near us—thus I cried:
' Give o'er the conflict! Bootless is this war:
Would God we battled in the Holy Land
For freeing of Christ's Tomb!' Then answer'dst thou:
' Best of Crusaders is that king who fights
To free his country slaved!'" Douglas replied,
"I said it, sire; God said it, too, and crowned you.
God, if He wills, can make you yet Crusader;
In death, Crusader—yea, or after death."
    The King sighed slightly, and his eyelids sank;
Again he spake, though now with wandering mind:
"Randolph was there. Rightly thou saved'st his honour,
Though breaking thus the mandate of thy king.
Ah me! All earthly honour is but jest."
Later his eyes unclosed; and with strong voice
And hand half raised as if it grasped a sceptre
He spake: "My youthful dream is unfulfilled--
That sin I sinned when Comyn died forbade it:
Not less one tribute I would pay to God,
Leave man one fair ensample.
Yon case of silver is a reliquary—
Seal thou therein my heart when dead I lie:
In the Holy Land inter it."
                    Three weeks passed,
Five ships were freighted, and the Douglas sailed,
Bearing that reliquary on his breast
Both day and night. He fared not forth alone,
For lords as many companied him as sailed
With good Sir Patrick Spens, what time he bore

Scotland's fair daughter, " Maid of Norway" named,
To be the North-King's bride. Those lords of old
Saw never more their native land.   They died—
Died at the feet of that sea-warrior grey
When, tempest-wrecked on their return, their bark
Went down 'mid roaring waves.   Tempest as fierce
On the head of Douglas broke.   A Spanish port
With inland-winding bosom bright and still
Received him ; and Alphonso of Castile
Welcomed, well pleased, with tournament and feast
A guest in all lands famed.
     The parting day
Had almost come ; disastrous news foreran it.
 Granada's Sultan with his Saracen host
Had broken bound, and written on his march
His Prophet's name in fire.   Alphonso craved
Aid of his guest.   In sadness Douglas mused ;
At last he spake : " Sir King, unblest is he
That knight whom warring duties rend asunder :
My King commanded me to Palestine !
For thirty days that word was in mine ears
'Neath all our festal songs.   A deeper voice
Assails me now, mounting from that great Heart
Shrined on this breast.   Thus speaks it : ' That command
I gave thee knowest thou not I countermand—
I who from righteous battle ne'er turned back ?' "
The Douglas drooped his head ; a trumpet-peal
Shrilled from afar.   He raised that head ; he spake :
" Alphonso of Castile, my choice is made ;
With thee I march !"   The Scottish knights drew swords,
Shouted " Saint Andrew !" and the knights of Spain
Made answer, " Santiago !"
     Long or e'er
The next sun rose, and while the morning star
Saw still its own face glassed in eastern seas,
Its radiance saw flashed from the floods, that, swollen
By melting snows, thundered through dark ravines—

As brightly flashed as e'er from Cedron's stream
Or Siloa's sacred wave—in that fair hour
The hosts united marched. Ere long they met
On a wide plain with white sierras girt
The Prophet's sons, for centuries their foes.
The Moors were to the Christians three to one.
For hours that battle-storm was heard afar;
Numbers at last prevailed; and on the left
The standard of the Cross some whit lost ground :
Douglas restored the battle. On the right
His Scottish knights and he drove all before them.
The Moors gave way ; fleet were their Arab steeds,
And better than their foes they knew the ground.
Far off they formed anew ; they waved again
Their moonéd flags, and crescent scimitars
Well used to reap the harvest-fields of death.
Once more they shouted "Allah !"   Spent and breathless,
The Northern knights drew bridle on a slope
A stone's-throw distant. Douglas shouted, " Forward !"
None answered. Sadly—not in wrath—he spake :
" O friends, how oft on stormy war-fields proved !
This day what lack ye ? Naught save an example !"
Forward he spurred ; he reached the Saracen van ;
He raised on high that silver shrine ; he cried,
" Go first, great Heart, as thou wert wont to go ;
Douglas will follow thee and die."   He flung it :
Next moment he was in among the Moors.
The Scots knights heard that word ; they saw ; they charged.
Direful the conflict; from a hill Alphonso
Watched it, but, pressed himself, could spare no aids :
He sent them when too late.

                        The setting sun
Glared fiercely at that fugitive Moorish host;
Shone sadly on that remnant, wounded sore,
Which gazed in circle on their Great One dead.
His hands, far-stretched, still grappled at the grass :

His bosom on that silver shrine was pressed :
His last hope this—to save it.
　　　　　　　　They returned,
That wounded remnant, to their country's shores :
With them they bore the Bruce's Heart; yet none
Sustained it on his breast.　In season due
The greatest and the best of Scotland's realm,
Old lords high-towered on river-banks tree-girt,
Old Gaelic chiefs that ruled in patriarch state
The blue glens of that never-vanquished land,
Grave shepherd-prelates, guiding with mild awe
Those flocks Iona's sons had given to Christ,—
In sad procession moved with sacred rites
From arch to arch of Melrose's holy pile
Following King Robert's Heart before them borne
'Neath canopy of gold, and there interred it
Nigh the high altar.　Peasants pressed around
Countless that hour.　Some whispered, "Meet it was
Here, in this place, to inter our Robert's Heart;
For though he never fought in Holy Land—
He might not, since for our sake God forbade it—
That heart was a Crusader's."　James of Douglas,
In later ages named "the Good Earl James,"
Was buried in the chancel of Saint Bride's
Near his ancestral castle.　Since that day
The Douglas shield has borne a Bleeding Heart
Crowned with a kingly crown.
　　　　　　　　There are who say
That on the battle-morn, but ere the bird
Of morn had flung far off that clarion peal
Which chides proud boastings and denial base,
King Robert stood beside the Douglas' bed
With face all glorious, like some face that saith
"True friends on earth divided meet in heaven."

ALFRED TENNYSON.

NONE sang of love more nobly; few as well;
Of Friendship, none with pathos so profound;
Of Duty, sternliest proved when myrtle-crowned;
Of English grove and rivulet, mead and dell;
Great Arthur's Legend he alone dared tell;
Milton and Dryden feared to tread that ground;
For him alone o'er Camelot's faery bound
The "horns of Elf-land" blew their magic spell.
Since Shakespeare and since Wordsworth none hath sung
So well his England's greatness; none hath given
Reproof more fearless or advice more sage:
None inlier taught how near to earth is heaven;
With what vast concords Nature's harp is strung;
How base false pride; faction's fanatic rage.

Katharine Tynan.

(MRS. HINKSON.)

THERE are few names more familiar to readers of Irish literature than that of Katharine Tynan, who, by her recent marriage to a distinguished graduate of Trinity College, has now become Mrs. Hinkson. She is a native of the city of Dublin, and was educated at the Dominican Convent, Drogheda. After her studies had been completed there she returned home, and the next ten or twelve years of her life were spent in her father's picturesque home at Clondalkin, one of the charming suburbs of Dublin. Mr. Tynan is a farmer noted for his systematic and scientific methods of agriculture, and his farm has scarcely a rival for beauty and fertility in the whole province of Leinster. The following graphic picture of the early home of this talented authoress written some time ago by Mr. Eugene Davis will be interesting :—" The farmstead is a neat, trim cottage half hidden in clusters of clambering vines and clinging ivy intertwined with myrtles. Within, everything denotes comfort, taste, and neatness. Miss Tynan's boudoir, where she penned all the volumes that have already been published, looks like a blended repository of art and letters. Pictures and books line its dainty walls. A portrait of the young hostess by the father of another young poet, Mr. W. B. Yeats, is a faithful reproduction on canvas of her face and figure, of her large pensive eyes, and wavy auburn tresses. Clondalkin, which will ever remain associated with Miss Tynan's literary career, is a romantic and historic spot."

Mrs. Hinkson's first published poem appeared in the *Graphic*, and her first volume was issued in the year 1885. "Louise de la Valliere and Other Poems" was the title of it. This work was a brilliant success and immediately brought her into prominence as a poetess of fertile imagination and rich descriptive powers. In 1887 appeared her second volume, entitled "Shamrocks," and in 1892 her "Ballads and Lyrics."

The graceful and facile pen of this sweetly singing poetess is ever busy, and she is as much at home in the field of graphic prose as she is well known to be in that of poetry. She is a favourite contributor to *The Speaker*, the *Westminster Budget*, the *National Observer*, *The Bookman*, and *Sylvia's Journal*. She is also literary critic and book-reviewer for the *Irish Daily Independent*, and is engaged in supplying an American syndicate with articles on current literary topics. She is a great admirer of the policy of the late Mr. Parnell, and at his death she wrote a poetical tribute to his memory, entitled, "The Dead Chief," which takes rank among the best elegies in the language. The fourth volume of her poetical works is entitled "Cuckoo Songs." It has just been published in an exquisite limited edition by Messrs. Elkin, Matthews, & Lane. The specimens we give are from this work.

SINGING STARS.

"What sawest thou, Orion, thou hunter of the star-lands,
    On that night star-sown and azure when thou cam'st in splendour sweeping
And amid thy starry brethren from the near lands and the far lands
    All the night above a stable on the earth thy watch wert keeping?"

" Oh, I saw the stable surely, and the young child and the mother,
   And the placid beasts still gazing with their wild eyes full of
   loving.
And I saw the trembling radiance of the Star, my lordliest brother,
   Light the earth and all the heavens as he kept his guard
   unmoving.

There were kings that came from Eastward with their ivory,
   spice and sendal,
   With gold fillets in their dark hair, and gold broidered robes
   and stately,
And the shepherds gazing star-ward, over yonder hill did wend all,
   And the silly sheep went meekly, and the wise dog marvelled
   greatly,

Oh, we knew, we stars, the stable held our King, His glory shaded,
   That His baby hands were poising all the spheres and con-
   stellations;
Berenice shook her hair down, like a shower of star dust braided,
   And Arcturus, pale as silver, bent his brows in adorations.

The stars sang altogether, sang their love-songs with the angels,
   With the Cherubim and Seraphim their shrilly trumpets blended,
They have never sung together since that night of great evangels,
   And the young Child in the manger, and the time of bondage
   ended."

THE STORY OF BLESSED COLUMBA AND THE HORSE.

COLUMBA was kept back
   Four years from his reward,
The brethren's prayers, alack,
   Prevailing with the Lord.
" O children, let me go ! "
   'Twas oft and oft he prayed,
Yet still with prayer aglow
   They held him from the dead.

They held him back with might,
  Kissing his habit's hem,
His soul's wings set for flight,
  Were prisoned long by them.
His soul was sick for death ;
  Yea, anguished long and dumb
To take the lonely path
  Should lead the exile home.

At last one Autumn day
  When woods were red and gold,
And the sea moaned alway
  For summers dead and cold,
Columba, weary foot,
  Went out and saw the sheaves,
And flames of yellow fruit
  Trembling among the leaves.

He saw the sheep and swine,
  The oxen and the ass,
The drying swathes in line
  Of rich and honeyed grass :
Opened the granary door,
  And saw the brethren had
Of fruit and grain great store
  To last through winter sad.

Upon a brother's arm
  The great Columba leant;
Bowed was that stately form,
  The holy head down-bent.
Yet peace was in his eyes,
  Happy and satisfied :
He blessed the granaries,
  The beasts and pastures wide.

As slowly home they came,
  There limped along the road,
The old horse tired and lame
  That long had borne his load.

The horse that night and morn
Drew home the abbey milk,
Drew home the load of corn,
And swathes of grass like silk.

With a low whinnying neigh,
He ran full wild and fast
And hid his forehead grey
Against Columba's breast,
And wept against his neck,
Till any heart of stone
Were very like to ache,
Hearing the creature moan.

"O little horse, so kind"
The dear Columba said;
"How hast thou well divined
I should so soon be dead?
Thou wouldst not keep me, thou,
From glory and from grace
And from Queen Mary's brow,
And from the Lord God's face!"

But while the horse sobbed on,
Columba stroked his mane;
O, any heart of stone
Had ached to see that pain.
And still as home they went,
The horse came following yet;
His head deject and bent,
His eyes still strained and wet.

The brethren they ran out:
Columba, speaking then,
His tender arm about
His patient friend's grey mane.
"O kinder is the beast
That grieves, but lets me go,
Than ye who keep from rest
An old man, sad and slow!

" Far kinder is the horse :
   He knows how pastures dim,
With many a water-course,
   Beckon so sweet to him.
He too is tired and old,
   And knows how sweetly call
The harps and hymns of gold
   To me this evenfall.

" Long have they called to me,
   My soul is hungerèd
The dear Lord God to see,
   With glories round His head.
Sweet is the thought of rest,
   While all the ages roll,
In that eternal Breast :
   Yea, lovely to my soul !"

They cried then with one voice :
   " No more we will retard,
Go, elect soul, rejoice,
   Receive thy great reward !
And yet forget not there
   The little ones who go
Like some sad wayfarer
   When heaven lets out the snow !"

They led the horse away
   Unto his manger brown.
Three days the sorrel-gray
   Let the big tears fall down.
Three days the horse did mourn ;
   The fourth day dawn came faint :
Iona woke forlorn,
   But heaven received its saint.

Alfred Percebal Grabes.

MR. ALFRED PERCEVAL GRAVES belongs to a well-known Limerick family, many of whom are distinguished for their literary talent. His father, the Right Rev. Charles Graves, D.D., Bishop of Limerick, is one of the most scholarly ecclesiastics of the Church to which he belongs, and is a noted Irish antiquary; his uncle, the late Dr. Robert Perceval Graves, was a poet of note and the biographer of Sir William Rowan Hamilton. The two brothers of the poet, Mr. Arnold Graves, Dublin, and Mr. Charles L. Graves, London, are both well known in the literary world, the latter being author of "The Blarney Ballads" and "The Green Above the Red." The subject of this notice was born in Dublin, on 22nd July, 1846. The early part of his schooldays was spent in the English lake country where his uncle, the late Rev. R. Perceval Graves, LL.D., was a Church of England clergyman, and the intimate friend of Wordsworth, Mrs. Hemans, and others of the late poets. His school days over, Mr. Graves returned to Dublin and entered Trinity College. In the course of a very successful university career he obtained first-class honours in classics and English literature, won the University Scholarship of Classics, carried off the medal of the Philosophical Society for poetry, and graduated B.A. in 1871. During his college course he frequently wrote for *Kottabos* and the *University Magazine*. At the end of his university career, Mr. Graves obtained an appointment in the Home Office, London, and shortly afterwards became private

secretary to Mr. Henry Winterbotham, the Parliamentary
Under-Secretary to the Home Office. During this time
he was a contributor to several London magazines,
including *The Athenæum, The Gentleman's Magazine,
Punch,* and *The Spectator,* and acted as dramatic critic for
The Examiner.

In 1873 Mr. Graves collected his first volume. It
was entitled, "Songs of Killarney," and was dedicated to
his parents. This work met with an enthusiastic reception.
It was favourably noticed by the press in England,
Ireland, and America, and brought the author compli-
mentary commendations from such distinguished *litterateurs*
and critics as Tennyson, Sir Samuel Ferguson, Charles
Lever and Professor Dowden. "Irish Songs and Ballads"
appeared in 1882. It was dedicated to Dr. R. P. Graves,
whom he describes as the indulgent critic of his boyish
verses and the helpful counsellor of his early manhood.
Like its predecessor, it ran through several editions, and
is now out of print. "Father O'Flynn and other Irish Lyrics"
(Swan, Sonnerschein & Co.) was issued in 1889. It is a
selection from his previously published works. Of this
collection a critic says:—"Mr. Graves gives us many
tender and idyllic pictures of peasant life in Ireland,
and the intimate knowledge he displays of the loves and
sorrows, the thoughts and feelings of the Irish peasant,
and their melodious *patois* or dialect, are the result of a profound, but above all, sympathetic study of the curious, and
many sided characteristics, and uncertain and wayward
ways of the inhabitants of the hills and valleys of the south
of Ireland. All the phases of Irish life, the lights and
shadows are here depicted with the touch of the true
poet, who sees things not visible to the common ken, and
invests with a living interest what would otherwise

appear to be the most commonplace of things." Some
time ago a collection of some fifty of Mr. Graves' lyrics
set to music—old Irish airs—harmonized by Dr. Charles
Villiers Stanford, was published by Messrs. Boosey & Co.
"Father O'Flynn" appeared in this collection. Mr.
Santley, the great English baritone, took a fancy to the
words and tune, and sang it at one of Boosey's ballad
concerts where it was received with the greatest enthusiasm, the distinguished singer having been recalled no
less than four times by the enraptured audience. Mr.
Graves has edited "Songs of Irish Wit and Humour,"
and "The Purcell Papers," a collection of Irish Stories,
and is now engaged in preparing a collection of "Irish
Songs and Airs" for the New Irish Library, edited by
Sir Charles Gavan Duffy. He is Honorary Secretary to the Irish Literary Society of London, in the
success of which he takes a deep and practical interest.
He is an authority on ancient bardic literature. In
January of the present year (1894) at the invitation of
the Royal Institution of Great Britain he gave a lecture
on "Old Irish Song" in London. The lecture was
vocally illustrated by Miss Liza Lehmann and Mdmlle.
Marie Bréma, the leading idyllic and the foremost
dramatic singer of the day, from "Songs of Old Ireland"
and "Irish Songs and Ballads," a collection of Mr.
Graves' lyrics written to old Irish airs, arranged by Dr.
Stanford, and published by Novello & Co. Both
lecture and songs were greeted with the heartiest applause
by the large and critical West End audience. In this
and other ways Mr. Graves has done much to popularize
Irish songs in the English metropolis. The works of no
Irish poet are more intensely Irish than that of the author
of "Father O'Flynn," and his love for his native land is

embodied in many of his compositions. The sentiment
of the Irish people has never been interpreted more
tenderly, more sympathetically, or more touchingly, than
in the following lines from "The Exiles":—

O, if for every tender tear
　　That from our aching, exiled eyes
Has fallen for you, Erin dear,
　　Our own lov'd shamrocks could arise,
They'd weave and weave a garland green
　　To stretch the cruel ocean through,
All, all the weary way between
　　Our yearning Irish hearts and you.

And oh! if every patriot prayer,
　　Put forth for your sad sake to God,
Could in one cloud of incense rare
　　Be lifted o'er your lovely sod,
That cloud would curtain all the skies
　　That far and near your fairness cope,
Until upon its arch of sighs
　　There beamed Heaven's rainbow smile of hope.

FATHER O'FLYNN.

OF priests we can offer a charmin' variety,
Far renowned for larnin' and piety;
Still, I'd advance ye, widout impropriety,
　　Father O'Flynn as the flower of them all.

　　Chorus – Here's a health to you, Father O'Flynn,
　　　　*Slainté,** and *slainté*, and *slainté* agin;
　　　　　Powerfulest preacher, and
　　　　　Tinderest teacher, and
　　　　Kindliest creature in ould Donegal.

---

* Your health.

Don't talk of your Provost and Fellows of Trinity,
Famous for ever at Greek and Latinity,
Dad and the divels and all at Divinity,
   Father O'Flynn 'd make hares of them all!
Come, I vinture to give ye my word,
Never the likes of his logic was heard,
     Down from mythology
     Into thayology,
  Troth! and conchology if he'd the call.
     Chorus—Here's a health to you, Father O'Flynn,
       Slainté, and *slainté*, and *slainté* agin;
       Powerfulest preacher, and
       Tinderest teacher, and
       Kindliest creature in ould Donegal.

Och! Father O'Flynn, you've the wonderful way wid you,
All ould sinners are wishful to pray wid you,
All the young childer are wild for to play wid you,
   You've such a way wid you, Father avick!
Still, for all you've so gentle a soul,
Gad, you've your flock in the grandest control;
     Checking the crazy ones,
     Coaxin' onaisy ones,
  Liftin' the lazy ones on wid the stick.
     Chorus—Here's a health to you, Father O'Flynn,
       Slainté, and *slainté*, and *slainté* agin;
       Powerfulest preacher, and
       Tinderest teacher, and
       Kindliest creature in ould Donegal.

And though quite avoidin' all foolish frivolity,
Still at all seasons of innocent jollity,
Where was the play-boy could claim an equality
   At comicality, Father, wid you?
Once the Bishop looked grave at your jest,
Till this remark set him off wid the rest:
     "Is it lave gaiety
     All to the laity?
  Cannot the clargy be Irishmen too?"

Chorus – Here's a health to you, Father Ó'Flynn,
· *Slainté*, and *slainté*, and *slainté* agin ;
Powerfulest preacher, and
Tinderest teacher, and
Kindliest creature in ould Donegal. ·

THE LIGHT IN THE SNOW.

OH, Pat, the bitter day when you bravely parted from us,
The mother and myself on the cruel quays of Cork :
When you took the long kiss, and you gave the faithful promise
That you'd soon bring us over to be wid you at New York.

But the times they grew worse through the wild, weary winter,
And my needle all we had to find livin' for us two ;
While the mother drooped and drooped till I knelt down forenint her
And closed her dyin' eyes, dear,—but still no word of you.

Then the neighbours thought you false to me, but I knew you better,
Though the bud became the leaf, and the corn began to start ;
And the swallow she flew back, and still sorra 'letter ;
But I sewed on and on, Pat, and kep' a stout heart.

Till the leaves they decayed, and the rook and the starlin'
Returned to the stubble ; and I'd put by enough
To start at long last in search of my darlin',
Alone across the ocean so unruly and rough.

Until at the end, very weak and very weary,
I reached the overside, and started on my search ;
But no account for ever of Patrick for his Mary,
By advertisin' for you, dear, or callin' you in church.

Yet still I struggled on, though my heart was almost broken
· And my feet torn entirely on the rough, rugged stone ;
Till that day it came round, signs by and by token,
The day five year that we parted you, mavrone.

Oh! the snow it was sweepin' through the dark, silent city,
  And the cruel wind it cut through my thin, tattered gown;
Still I prayed the good God on his daughter to take pity;
  When a sudden strange light shone forenint me up the town.

And the light it led on till at last right opposite
  A large, lonely house it vanished as I stood;
Wid my heart axing wildly of me, was it, oh, was it
  A warnin' of ill or a token of good?

Then the light kindled up agin, brighter and bigger,
  And I saw my own shadow across the window cast,
While close, close, and closer to it stole a man's figure,
  And I fainted, as you caught me in your true arms at last.

Then Pat, my own Pat, I saw that you were altered
  To the shadow of yourself by the fever on the brain!
While "Mary, Mary darlin'," at last your lips they faltered,
  "You've given your poor Patrick his mem'ry back again."

And the good, gentle priest, when he comes, is never weary
  Of sayin', as he spakes of that light in the snow,
"The Lord heard your prayer, and in pity for you, Mary,
  Restored Pat the raison that he lost long ago."

THE LITTLE RED LARK.

O SWAN of slenderness,
Dove of tenderness,
  Jewel of joys, arise!
The little red lark,
Like a soaring spark
  Of song, to his sun-burst flies.
But till thou art risen,
Earth is a prison
  Full of my lonesome sighs;
Then awake and discover
To thy fond lover
  The morn of thy matchless eyes!

The dawn is dark to me,
Hark! O, hark to me,
    Pulse of my heart, I pray!
And out of thy hiding
With blushes gliding,
    Dazzle me with thy day.
Ah, then once more to thee
Flying I'll pour to thee
    Passion so sweet and gay,
The lark shall listen,
And dew-drops glisten
    Laughing on every spray.

THE FOGGY DEW.

OH! a wan cloud was drawn
O'er the dim, weeping dawn,
    As to Shannon's side I returned at last;
And the heart in my breast
For the girl I loved best
    Was beating, ah, beating how loud and fast!
While the doubts and the fears
Of the long, aching years
    Seemed mingling their voices with the moaning flood;
Till full in my path,
Like a wild water wraith,
    My true love's Shadow lamenting stood.

But the sudden sun kissed
The cold, cruel mist
    Into dancing showers of diamond dew;
The dark flowing stream
Laughed back to his beam,
    And the lark soared singing aloft in the blue;
While no phantom of night,
But a form of delight
    Stood with arms outspread for her darling boy;
And the girl I love best
On my wild throbbing breast
    Hid her thousand treasures with a cry of joy.

Harriet Glasgow Acheson.

MRS. HARRIET G. ACHESON is daughter of the late Rev. Professor Glasgow, D.D., pioneer missionary to Gujarat, India. She was educated, for a time, at Walthamstow, and afterwards at the Victoria College, Belfast. When very young—even before she left school— she began to compose verse, and her first published poem appeared in " M'Comb's Almanack " for 1867. Mr. M'Comb was well known as a poet in his day, and his name is still fresh in the memory of a large section of the Ulster public. He recognised the ability of the young poetess, and the appreciation which he showed of her contributions encouraged her greatly. She was afterwards of much service to him in the compilation of his popular annual during his declining years.

In 1877 she was married to John Acheson, Esq., J.P., Portadown.

Mrs. Acheson is a fluent, vigorous, and graceful writer, both in prose and poetry. She is a warm advocate of Temperance, and makes herself acquainted with the current public questions of the day, including land reform, on which she has written a series of ballads that have enjoyed much popularity. They were first published in the *Lurgan Times*, and were reprinted in at least seven newspapers across the Channel. They have since been published in a collected form. She wrote two continued stories for *Daybreak*—" Frank's Little Mother" and " A Different Girl"—and a serial for *The Presbyterian Church-man*. Poems from her pen have frequently appeared in these magazines. She wrote a short story in verse for the

Witness, entitled "Essie's Gold," which was very popular. The best of her poetical works is a temperance story-poem entitled "Willie's Quest," recently published by the Religious Tract Society. It is a pathetic tale, in which the evils of intemperance are depicted with great vigour, in easy flowing verse.

MARRY A FARMER! NO!

MARRY a farmer, Jenny!
  Not with my will, my lass;
Your father will lie in the churchyard
  Before that comes to pass.
To think of you living a lifetime
  Of drudgery and care,
With never an hour of leisure,
  With never a coin to spare;
Moiling and toiling, Jenny,
  As your mother did with me—
As I seek your good, my daughter,
  I cannot let it be.
You say that John has happened
  On land with an easy rent;
The place is out of order,
  But you can be content;
Your John is strong and steady,
  And does not shrink from toil;
His skill and honest labor
  Will work wonders on the soil.
All very true, my lassie —
  John is a clever lad—
That does not mend the matter,
  It makes it twice as bad.
I'll tell you what will happen
  When yonder bare hillside
Is clad with waving golden grain,
  Your husband's joy and pride:

He will find himself the poorer
  For all the labour spent,
For richer land, the agent says,
  MUST PAY A HIGHER RENT.
Don't cry, my little Jenny,
  It is no time for tears,
Young heads had need be cool and wise,
  For these are evil years !
Young hearts had need be proof against
  The sweetest dreams of life,
If they do not wish to be beaten down
  In the hard and bitter strife.
Don't cry, don't cry, my Jenny !
  It almost breaks my heart
To see you weep so bitterly :
  But I must do my part.
Listen to me, my daughter—
  God knows I speak in love—
I think if your mother looks on us
  From her happy rest above,
She will know that it is no selfishness
  Which makes me thwart your will,
But the bitter memories of my life
  That linger with me still.
I am an old and broken man,
  Wound in a mesh of debt.
I once could boast an honest name,
  And I am honest yet ;
But there are men I cannot meet
  Without a blush of shame ;
The blot of debt he cannot pay
  Has marred your father's fame.
I gave good heed to barn and field :
  Your mother toiled and slaved !
We neither drank nor spent amiss,
  And when we could we saved ;
We did not grumble at our lot,
  Our hearts and hands were strong ;

We trusted that the hardest toil
  Would not be needed long;
That when old age came creeping on,
  Our children would be there
To cheer our hearts with grateful love,
  To lighten work and care.
Our hopes grew brighter as the land
  Grew better year by year;
We had a peaceful, happy home,
  But evil days were near!
You know the rest. The years had flown,
  At last the lease was up;
And then there come the bitterest drop
  In all our bitter cup:
The land was better, so they said,
  And claimed a higher rent.
I took my burden patiently,
  And tried to be content;
But when I sent your brothers forth
  To till a freer soil,
And when I saw your mother die,
  Worn out with grief and toil,—
I felt that I could hardly bear
  The burden of the years:—
One sacred duty still was left,
  To save my child from tears.
Come, Jenny, be a woman, lass!
  And face your trouble well,
Perchance new times may bring new laws
  And better, who can tell?
Meantime, you have your brothers, Jane,—
  I have not long to stay—
They kept the wolf from off our door
  Through many a weary day.
They'll shield your life from want and care;
  Your heart will learn content—
But marry a farmer, Jenny!
  No, not with my consent!

ON THE LOSS OF MRS. BEATTY AND DR. MARY MacGEORGE IN THE S.S. "ROUMANIA."

O GOD, we bow beneath thy stroke,
  Thy people's first despairing "Why?"
Is hushed—it was the Master spoke
  In the wild gale and tempest high.

The Lord who calmed the sudden wave
  For trembling hearts on Galilee,
Still swift to hear, and strong to save,
  Was there amid the raging sea.

And when they cried—for life was dear—
  An answer fast their hopes was given,
"Come home! Your harbour is not here:
  Ye ask for earth; I give you heaven."

But to our eyes the glory's veiled;
  That shore seems far, a vision dim;
We can but think of hopes that failed
  When sorrow stilled faith's soaring hymn.

The clouded homes, the hearts that bleed,
  The Church's courts with mourners filled,
These are our share: the heathen's need
  Calls for the labourers brave and skilled.

Yet still the Lord Jehovah reigns,
  And he whose grace was strong in these
Can call from Erin's hills and plains
  A host to serve Him if He please.

Can make our mourning Zion rise
  With love new-kindled, sorrow-stirred,
Can bid her view with startled eyes
  The heathen waiting for the Word.

HOPE.

(Heb. vi., 17-19.)

I.

When clouds hang darkest on our way,
    One star serene
That tells of worlds of perfect day,
    Smiling is seen,
The Father knows what sorrows rise
    Like tempests dread;
He knows the tears that dim our eyes,
    Sees the bowed head.
He cannot leave his children thus
    In dark despair;
" Let there be light," He says, for us,
    And Hope is there.
That radiant star can pierce the gloom
    Of sorrow's night,
And trace thro' shadows of the tomb
    A path of light.

II.

God cannot see our bark too long
    By rude winds driven,
So from His hands secure and strong
    Our anchor's given.
Our faith so weak, its hold so slight,
    Can God forgive?
He only longs to chase our night
    And bid us live.
Oh! condescension undeserved,
    Love that brims o'er—
We doubt His word, He has reserved
    Yet one plea more—
" My word immutable ye doubt,
    Mine oath shall plead,"
Lord, can we shut Thy pity out
    And take no heed?

Thy love thus yearning for our love
Conquers our heart ;
Faith rises all our doubts above,
Our God Thou art !
Let storm-clouds gather like a pall
From East to West,
Our souls will let Thine anchor fall
And find their rest.

Rev. S. K. Wills, M.A.

THE Rev. Canon Wills is well and favourably known throughout the South of Ireland as a fluent, graceful, and versatile writer, both in prose and poetry. The following are some of the publications of which he is author : "Affection's Tribute," "Childhood," "Influence," "Lord Eldon," "Wellington" (dedicated by permission to H.R.H. the Duke of Connaught), and "Kilkee." This last work is considered by many his worthiest contribution to English literature. It is a poem of 134 stanzas, in which he describes in bold and eloquent language every place of interest in and around that famous and justly celebrated watering-place. It " gives evidence of his delight in the beauties of nature, while at the same time it contains faithful descriptive work. The journey from Limerick, the struggle at Kilrush, the hotels, the houses, the shops of Kilkee, and the natural scenery lovingly pourtrayed—the whole interspersed with moralizings, criticisms, and reflections on such subjects as temperance, music, &c. A more charming *souvenir* of a charming watering-place can scarcely be found than the poem ' Kilkee.' "

Canon Wills was educated at Trinity College, Dublin, where he graduated M.A. in 1858. After receiving holy orders he was appointed to the curacy of Parsonstown, where he spent the first twelve years of his ministerial life, and for the next six years was Vicar of Sixmile-bridge, Co. Clare. In 1872 he was appointed Rector of Rathkeale, Co. Limerick, where he has remained ever since. He is Rural Dean, Prebendary of St. Mary's Cathedral, and has been Chaplain to their Excellencies the Earls of Carnarvon, Zetland, and the Marquis of Londonderry. He was presented with a " Good Service Pension," not long since, by the Lord Bishop of Limerick. He is a favourite contributor to *Judy*, *Life*, *The Irish Ecclesiastical Gazette*, and poems from his pen on subjects of local interest appear from time to time in the columns of the provincial newspapers.

ST. MARY'S CATHEDRAL, LIMERICK.

I.

It is a sacred pile—hoary with age!
  Approach we its high courts, with rev'rent tread;
Let meaner thoughts no visitor engage
  As we survey the records of the dead,
And mark each granite vault and lowly bed,
  Where young and old in amity repose—
In calm serenity—in slumber dread,—
  Remov'd from earthly pains and cares and woes,
  And reckless of each blast, that o'er their ashes blows!

II.

Palace erewhile of Kings! Oh! could thy walls
  Speak of the past, what tidings should we glean

Of olden pomp and pageantry! Thy halls
  Were brilliant with full many a joyous scene,
Where youthful Beauty's ever radiant sheen
  Pour'd its fair light around; and every eye
Shone bright, and every happy heart, I ween,
  Throbb'd out its tale of love! Or if a sigh
Escap'd, 'twas grief that bliss like their's should ever die.

III.

Alas! the regal festivals are o'er
  Destroying Time hath laid the sceptre low,
That Donald wav'd upon fam'd Shannon's shore;
  Shiver'd his lance is—broken is his bow—
The jousts—the princely tournaments, that so
  Rejoic'd the spirits in the days of old,
Are all forgotten, like the dead below —
  The fair, the lov'd, the pure, the true, the bold—
Alike evanish'd now—blent in one common mould!

IV.

And when revolving years had o'er thee sped,
  What horrors rag'd around thy classic tow'rs!
Red Battle rear'd aloft its sanguine head,
  Yet thou didst stand amid conflicting pow'rs,
Like some grim sentinel! When iron show'rs
  Burst fiercely on thee thou didst, still unmov'd,
Toll from thy height the long, successive hours;
  And, though the cannon's rain thy walls had groov'd,
Thou didst not fail—and thus thou hast thy prowess prov'd!

V.

Historic Fane! Involved in many a change,
  And yet surviving! O'er thy varied stage
What diverse scenes have swept! How weird and strange,
  Could we now trace them all on Hist'ry's page!
Methinks it were fit study to engage
  A thoughtful mind, to trace each time worn stone,—
To note each Prince, Divine, Soldier or Sage
  That was, in union with thy glories, known—
Yes! let me muse upon it all, here, and—alone!

VI.

Alone—yet not alone!--the very air
  Seems charter'd with the spirits of the past!
And as I think upon the annals rare—
  The chequer'd story—all the int'rests vast
Bound with thy fortune from the first to last,
  I love thee more than ever! And whene'er
Death, with his spell, these eyeballs shall o'ercast,
  I'll fondly turn to thee, and breathe a pray'r
  To meet above, the souls that, with me, worshipp'd there.

VII.

Ah! yes, thou art—hast been for many a year,
  Our hallow'd Mother Church! - where oft have trod
The feet of prelates, priests, and people dear,
  Who now sleep on the bosom of their God!
Thou grand old temple! May each sacred sod
  Within thy bounds be honour'd evermore!
May no disaster—no afflictive rod,
  Its chastisement, again, upon thee pour,
  Or rend thy peaceful haunts, as they were rent before!

VIII.

Long may'st thou raise thy massive tow'rs on high!
  Long may the truth from out thy pulpit sound!
Long may thy choir pour forth "deep harmony,"
  And thy loud pealing organ swell around!
May fervent worshippers, still more abound,
  And all thy faithful clergy daily see
Good cause to hope there shall, at last, be found
  Amongst their people, who, *there*, bend the knee,
  Full many priceless souls, saved for Eternity!

GOOD-BYE!

" Et vos valeatis, Amici." *Propertius.*

HOW short! how simple!—yet how much
　Lies hid beneath *that* word!
How often has its magic touch
　　Wak'd a responsive chord,
　　　And flooded the whole heart with woe—
　　　The heritage of all below.

"Good-bye!" oft trembles on the lip
　Of friends approved and dear,—
When hands are locked in closest grip,
　　When falls devotion's tear;
　　　When swells the breast with many a sigh—
　　　Yes! there is pain in that "Good-bye!"

"Good-bye!" The gentle brother speaks,
　As, at his sister's side,
He stands, with blanch'd and moisten'd cheeks,
　　And checks the rising tide
　　　Of deep, fraternal sympathy—
　　　How tender is that soft "Good-bye!"

"Good-bye!" the loving mother says,
　As to her breaking heart
She folds her child, and fondly prays
　　That, though they now must part,
　　　They'll meet again, above the sky—
　　　Most sacred is that sad "Good-bye!"

"Good-bye!" the husband, or the wife,
　In Death's supreme embrace,
Gasps forth—last flickering of life!—
　　Ere stillness seals the face,
　　　And stops the pulse, and shrouds the eye—
　　　There's anguish in that dread "Good-bye!"

" Good-bye!"   Ah! what a world of pain
Exists when hearts that burn'd
With mutual love grow cold again,
By pique, or interest, turn'd !
There's nought more bitter than the cry
Of rent affection's last " Good-bye!"

" Good-bye!"   Oh! word of vast extent!
Let us thy meaning learn —
'Tis " *God be with you !*"—So, when spent
With grief, and when we yearn
For parting friends, look we on high,
And pray for each—" Good-bye! Good-bye!"

PASSING AWAY.

WHEN the star of Hope is brightest,
And the heart most full of joy,—
When the spirits bound the lightest,
And the bliss knows no alloy -
Then, perchance, the smiling river
Of our pleasures ends for ever !

Often have we seen the morning
Glow resplendent, balmy, fair—
Mountain, plain, and vale adorning,
Fragrance filling all the air,
And soon found the lightning flashing,
And the angry thunders crashing !

Often have we mark'd, unbroken,
Ocean's bosom, broad and calm,
And have own'd a joy, unspoken,
'Mid still Nature's soothing balm,—
But anon, the waters sleeping,
Rag'd, beneath the tempests' sweeping !

Often have we known the fairest,
  Mark'd with purity and grace—
Gifted with endowments rarest,
  Faultless, both in form and face—
Yet collapse, before the blighting
Of decay, in silence smiting!

Calm repose, and classic feature,
  Lustrous eye, and clust'ring hair,—
Paragon—'twould seem—of Nature,
  Moulded softly, sweetly fair!
Oh! how often has Death parted
Us from such—half broken-hearted!

Thus it has been! Thus, for ever,
  Must it be, until we gain
That eternal shore, where never
  Change can come, nor tears, nor pain,—
Where from trouble there is ceasing,
From Time's severings releasing.

G. F. Savage-Armstrong, D.Lit.

MR. GEORGE FRANCIS SAVAGE-ARMSTRONG, (born May 5, 1845,) is the only surviving son of the late Edmund J. Armstrong, Esq., a descendant of the old and celebrated Border stock of the Armstrongs of Liddesdale, and his wife, Jane, last surviving daughter of the Rev. Henry Savage, of Glastry, J.P., Incumbent of Ardkeen, Co. Down, of the ancient and noble Anglo-Norman family of the Savages of Ardkeen and Portaferry, "the lords of the Ards." He represents the Glastry branch of the Savages of the Ards, and, consequent upon the death of a maternal uncle some years ago, assumed the additional surname of "Savage" prefixed to "Armstrong." From close family connection with both the northern and midland counties of Ireland, he is in all respects, perhaps, an "Anglo-Irishman." His elder brother, Edmund Armstrong, was the well-known Irish poet of precocious genius, who died at the age of 23, leaving behind him a poetical legacy which so keen a critic as Ste.-Beuve declared would hold a permanent place in the literature of England.

Mr. Savage-Armstrong's early years were spent in the southern side of the County of Dublin, and amongst the mountains and valleys of Wicklow, which he loved with an ardour that has never abated. Wordsworth himself could not have adored Nature more passionately or revelled in it with wilder intoxication than he did as a child. The love of Nature led, in his brother's case and in his, to the love of poetry; and in his boyhood both

were his daily food and drink. At the age of twelve he
had read all Shakespeare's plays and a vast deal of other
poetry and prose besides. He used to spend hours with a
book of poetry in his hand, in the tops of tall trees,
reading; or on the side of one of the Dublin or Wicklow
mountains, alone. Often also, along with his brother, he
would scale a mountain, with a volume of Byron, or Scott,
or Wordsworth, or Coleridge, or Keats, or Shelley, and
the two would lie in the heather reading alternately
poem after poem. Never did boys lead a more imaginative
life than did these two brothers, and their sympathy
with one another was perfect.

At the age of eleven he had written poems, which his
brother Edmund carefully and lovingly preserved for
many years, and which he used to point to with pride.
Yet, strange to say, his youthful ambition was to be a
soldier.

His early education was obtained at two different
day-schools which were then the principal ones in Dublin;
and there he showed a decided taste for the Classics and
for classical and English composition. At one of the
schools the Head Master made a point of retaining his
essays, to read them to his friends. But, on the whole,
the mountains and the fields and poetry drew him rather
away from systematic study. At this period his school
education was interrupted by his brother's illness, which
arrested the latter's brilliant University career, and he
accompanied his brother to the Channel Islands, where
again the boys' lives were lives of independent literary
study and thought, of imagination and romance. When
his brother was too ill for long walks, he used to ramble
about, reading, as he went along, Horace or Virgil or some
English or Italian poet, among the beautiful Jersey

orchards and by-roads; and when the invalid grew
stronger, the two would spend their days on the head-
lands, basking in the sunshine, reading or conversing, and
building up gorgeous dreams which were never to be
realised. During their stay in this island they received
good private teaching in Mathematics, French, and other
subjects.

When Edmund Armstrong's health was nearly re-
established, the brothers made excursions to Brittany and
Normandy; and they travelled on foot several hundred
miles through Normandy and other parts of France, and
visited Paris, living on 1 franc and 75 centimes per day
each, and sometimes less; and returned to Ireland with
a multitude of poetical impressions derived from the
cathedrals, the picturesque towns and villages, the
antiquities, and the people, of France.

When he returned to Ireland Mr. Savage-Armstrong
obtained, by competition, an official appointment in
Dublin, and immediately afterwards entered Trinity
College, where he at once began to take an active part in
the literary discussion of the Philosophical Society, in
which he won medals and prizes for essay-writing and
oratory, and of which he was subsequently elected to the
presidentship, which had been held by his brother, with
such marked distinction, for a few months before his
untimely death. His fellow-students of the Historical
and Philosophical Societies entrusted him with the duty
of editing the selection from his brother's poems, which
they, and some of the leading men of Dublin and of the
University, immediately published as a memorial of him.
Amongst other distinctions, he won the Vice-Chancellor's
prize of the University for poetry, at this time, and the
gold medal for composition of the Historical Society.

After his brother's death he ceased to reside within the walls of Trinity College, and for a year or two did not continue his University course. He loved to be alone; and, amongst other things, he walked by himself, with a knapsack on his back, through almost all the Northern counties of Ireland, thus making himself very familiar with the scenery and the people of Ulster, a province for which he has a strong partiality.

After resuming his University studies he was re-elected president of the Philosophical Society, and delivered the inaugural address, which was received with a more than usual amount of eulogy by the Press, the public, and the heads of the University. Before graduating, however, he went for a long tour through Germany, Switzerland, Italy, and France, most of it being accomplished in his usual way, on foot; and he brought out his first volume, "Poems : Lyrical and Dramatic" (the third edition of which was published some time ago) before taking his B.A. degree. This volume was excellently received. He now returned to the Continent, and spent a winter and spring rambling amidst the lovely scenery of the Riviera and the Maritime Alps; and, in the charming little Villa des Rosiers, in the Carrei Valley, at Mentone, he completed his Italian tragedy of *Ugone*, which was published in the following autumn. After another visit to Switzerland he returned to Dublin, and then went to reside in London, where he mixed much in intellectual circles, studied the stage, as it then was, with great care, and wrote occasionally for magazines, making, at intervals, rambles here and there in England.

The next event of importance in the poet's life was his appointment by the Crown to the Chair of English Literature in Queen's College, Cork, and to a Profes-

sorship in the late Queen's University. About this time
the Board of Trinity College presented him with his M.A.
degree, *stip. con*, in recognition of " high literary character and attainments." He threw himself into the work of
his Chair with enthusiasm, took a very active part in
encouraging intellectual activity and culture amongst the
students of Queen's College and the public, and delivered
many public lectures on literature and art to crowded
audiences ; and, in the meantime, wrote and published
his Hebrew Trilogy, " The Tragedy of Israel," and in
vacation-time travelled much in Italy and elsewhere.

This Trilogy was followed by his brother's " Life and
Letters " and a new edition of the latter's " Poetical
Works."

In 1879 Mr. Savage-Armstrong married Miss Marie
Elizabeth Wrixon, and in the same year he travelled very
extensively in Italy, Greece, Turkey, Austria, Germany,
and Holland ; and, as a fruit of his Greek rambles, he
published in the following year his volume of poems
entitled "A Garland from Greece," of which the King of
the Greeks expressed his cordial appreciation. This work
consists of poems dealing with the subjects of Greece
from many points of view—topographical, historical,
legendary, and political,—and in every case they are
treated with delicacy and taste.

Soon afterwards he was presented with the honorary
degree of Doctor-of-Literature by the Queen's University,
and a little later was elected a Fellow of the Royal
University.

Mr. Savage-Armstrong now returned to his first love,
and wrote " Stories of Wicklow," composing much of the
poetry on the summits of Slieve Cullen and other Wicklow
mountains, or in the recesses of the Wicklow woods and

glens. This is one of the best works of this eminent poet, and is, perhaps, better known than any other of his works. It is a volume of delightful poems, full of stately music, noble thoughts, and genuine passion ; and the rhyme and rhythm of the verse are always unexceptionable. Of these "Stories" a critic truthfully says— "The reader will find in them a charm that irresistibly allures him on from stanza to stanza. Mr. Armstrong ranks among the first of our living poets, and the reputation he has achieved is well sustained in these poems, which are rich in mellow harmonies, graceful rhymes, graphically drawn scenes full of swift and varied action, marked by the gloom of tragedy, the sunny rays of lighthearted joyousness, and the tenderest and sweetest pathos. He is a master of musical verse, and possesses that sympathy with man and nature without which no poet can move his reader to a common confession of joy or sorrow."

This work was followed by "Victoria Regina et Imperatrix : a Jubilee Song from Ireland," in 1887, for which her Majesty was graciously pleased to convey to him her thanks.

His next publication was "Mephistopheles in Broadcloth : a Satire" (1888), which hit so many people, and struck especially so hard at the literary cliques of London, that the reviewers were almost afraid to touch it. Until now Mr. Armstrong had not been known as a satirist, and the appearance of this work came like a thunderbolt to many who had read his previous publications. It dealt with Parliament, the Church, the Press, Art, Drama, Literature, and Fashion. The following press-notice fairly represents the character of the work :—"Never before has

Mr. Armstrong filled his poetic quiver with shafts of ridicule, but his supply is now large and complete, and the darts are driven with a precision that reaches their mark, and must arrest the admiration of even the passing observer. It is not a political manifesto. It is essentially a plea for Good in popular life—an argument for that conservatism of society which implies the greatest happiness of the greatest number, and an expression of the hopefulness of endeavour which is the very salt of the most wholesome satire. There are brilliant passages in the poem which Dryden might have penned in his easier moments. They are worth study and attention. They are close and keen in criticism, and elegantly ingenious in expression. They hit hard, yet fairly, and in the humour the element of dignity is not forgotten."

The next volume of poetry which Mr. Savage-Armstrong published was " One in the Infinite," a philosophical poem which deals with the deepest problems of the human mind. Perhaps no poem in the language covers such a wide intellectual field. It is written in a series of some two hundred and fourteen lyrics, varying according to the thought and emotion expressed, evolved one from the other, and constituting a single connected whole. By many people this work is regarded as the representative poem of the latter part of the nineteenth century.

When the Tercentenary of Dublin University was about to be celebrated, in 1892, the Board of Trinity College entrusted Mr. Savage-Armstrong with the very honourable duty of writing the Tercentenary Ode, which, set to the fine music of Sir Robert Prescott Stewart, was performed during the celebrations before an enormous audience with immense *éclat,* and was declared everywhere to constitute the great incident of the Tercentenary.

Besides many volumes of poems, various essays, and "The Life and Letters of Edmund J. Armstrong," this prolific writer has compiled (principally for private circulation) a large prose-work entitled "The Savages of the Ards," which is considered a valuable contribution to Ulster historical literature.

Mr. Savage-Armstrong spends a considerable portion of each year invariably in his much-loved County of Wicklow, where he has a pretty little place, commanding views of the lovely scenery which fascinated and inspired him in his childhood, and which is associated with the dearest and most exalting memories of his life.

THE SATYR.

I.

WAS he aweary of dancing in the woods
　　To Pan's wild fluting, when he drooped his head
　　Thus o'er his bosom, and his limbs outspread
Amid the rocks and piney solitudes,
　And fell a-dozing so deliciously?
　　Did some fantastic dæmon in the wine
　　Tangle his brain in such a sleepy twine,
And drench him with that quaint and drowsy glee?
　　Or drifted he to sleep with idle sails,
　　Charmed with witch lullabies of luscious nightingales?

II.

Blithe creature, in whose being meet and mingle
　　Man's motions with the life of dumb, dull things
　　Of field and thicket, and the spirit's wings
Half-fledged begin to pulsate and to tingle
With faint forefeelings of potential flights;
　　Dream of sin's soilure makes him not afraid;
　　No curb of Conscience on his heart is laid
To check his quickening senses' soft delights;
　　He roams the woods in measureless content,
　　Quaffing earth's mystic boons in pleased bewilderment.

III.

All rich and gummy odours soothe his sense ;
 All flavours of ripe berries in the brake,
 Or fruits that can the thirst of summer slake ;
All sounds of winds that come he knows not whence,
Whispering amid the tree-tops and the reeds,
 With bleat of sheep and low of uddered cows ;
 All glints of sunshine on the glossy boughs
And little leaflets bright with dewy beads ;
 The hornless kids that butt him, and the lambs
 That push against his knees and lick his clumsy palms.

IV.

But ah ! the vines. the vines in autumn's glow,
 With bloomy bunches trailing from the stem,
 What wooing witchery abides in them
That he should love to bask their boughs below
Like full-fed tortoise dozing in his shell,
 While o'er his breast and neck and visage brown
 Plump grapes and golden leaves come dropping down,
And all the air exhales a fruity smell,
 And every tendril tickling brows and nose
 Is as a touch of love to lull him to repose ?

V.

The trickling brook was dainty to his lip,
 But sure 'twas Bacchus' self, on frolic bent,
 That by the fount his thristy mates frequent
Laid once a beaker purple to the tip
With honeyed vintage tempting him to taste.
 Gods ! how he eyed the bright mysterious draught,
 Then took it timidly, and sipped, and laughed,
Then drained it to the lees in eager haste,
 Then laughed as if his joy could never fail,
 And like a dancing rivulet skipped adown the dale !

VI.

He nibbles the brown nuts with squirrel-mirth,
 And gambols kid-like through the rocky glades ;

He dances in the flickering olive-shades
To magic melodies of air and earth
That seize him with a reinless ecstasy,
    And whirl him leaping in fantastic round
    With jerking arms and feet that fly the ground;
While Pan, half hid in cave or hollow tree,
    Pursues him, while he pipes, with twinkling eyes,
    And holds his shaggy side for laughter as he flies.

VII.

In sooth he seems the sport of all the gods;
    Gay Eros hath bewildered his poor heart,
    And set him sighing for the nymphs that dart
With twinkling feet across the woodland sod;
For them he capers, smiles, and blithely sings;
    They flatter him with mischief in each eye;
    He fingers their smooth necks, and off they hie,
And round the rocks their mirthful laughter rings;
    Well pleased he laughs with them that laugh at him,
    And they forbear to chide a sense so vague and dim.

VIII.

Stop, and behold him as he dozes there,
    His listless limbs extended on the rock.
    Close by his side a goat from the black flock
Munches the ivy fallen from his hair;
The hornet whizzes harmless by; a bird
    With saffron breast beside an olive's root
    Drops down to peck the berries at his foot;
Because these two long hours he hath not stirred,
    The nightingale above him trills at ease,
    The lizard stares and pants, then climbs his gnarlëd knees.

IX.

He dreams of noonday slumbers as he sleeps,
    Of drowsy whispers in the waving tree,
    And far-off murmurs of the mystic sea,
And some soft eye that through the thicket peeps,

And glossy purring things that brush his palm,
And troops of laughing naiads at the spring
His face affrights amid their gambolling,
And white-necked dryads with their breath of balm,
And then of Bacchus and his purple wiles,
And, happier than a child, amid his sleep he smiles.
                    —*From "A Garland from Greece."*

IONIAN SERENADE.

THROUGH thy slumber softly stealing,
Lady, let my soul's appealing,
'Mid thy dreams my love revealing,
    O'er thy heart in music move.

Dream, O dream, that thou canst love me,
Dream that thou dost bend above me,
Murmuring, " Free thou art to love me,"
    Then awake, and *know* my love.

Wake, O wake, and hear my pleading;
At thy feet my life lies bleeding;
Hide not from mine eyes, unheeding,
    Lest before thy doors I die.

Rise, O rise, and draw thou near, love;
By thy lattice bend thine ear, love;
Thy poor lover, singing, hear, love,
    Lone beneath the midnight sky.

Ah, no more thy beauty screening,
From thy windows lightly leaning,
Hear, and learn my music's meaning,
    Hear and heed my whispered prayer!

Now the nightingales are sleeping,
While the lowly night-wind, sweeping,
Shows the stars in cluster peeping
    Through the pines that scent the air.

All the world in peace reposes;
E'en the loud cicala dozes
Where the luscious heavy roses
    Droop their blooms in dewy sleep.

Hist! by yonder mountain plashing,
Comes my little pinnace dashing,
Every lifted oar-blade flashing
    Fiery from the burning deep.

Where my bark 's at anchor riding,
O'er the bay the shadow 's gliding,
As the moon, her bright horn hiding,
    Drops adown by Daphne's crest.

Fly, and ere the dawn's upspringing,
Let the wind, in white sail singing,
O'er the waters fleetly winging,
    Waft thee to mine Island-nest!

Haste, O haste, that day may find thee,
Athens and thy foes behind thee,
While my arms from peril wind thee,
    Sailing fast by Hydra's side.

O, descend ere night be older!
Fold my cloak around thy shoulder.
Danger flies as Love grows bolder.
    Come, my darling, come, my bride.
        —From " A Garland from Greece."

NIGHT AND GOD.

(Extract from De Verdun of Darragh in " Stories of Wicklow.")

I.

O YE pine-woods in the moonlight high against the white clouds
    swaying,
  Tossed i' the warm and redolent tempest blowing over the
    moonlit sea,
How ye draw me from my doors, that I may hear the clear winds
    playing
  In your pungent plumy branches their tumultuous harmony,—

Treading here the tumbled cones amid the mossy woodland places,
  By my home upon the mountain where my rivulets leap and sing,
All the glory of night above me in the luminous sea-blue spaces,
  Flying mists and throbbing stars, that lift my spirit on aëry
    wing!

II.

Even now, within my chamber, o'er the Sage's volume bending,
  Dashed with sorrow, and troubled, brooding on the riddle of Life
    and God,
As I strained the aching brow, and, far my helpless hands extending,
  Groped amid the cavernous blackness, blind, with never a staff or
    rod,
Murmuring, Lo, of all his weary ceaseless toil is this the teaching—
  His, of living sons of men the amplest dowered with force and
    brain—
Only this—that soul and body are but one thing; this his
    preaching :—
  In the endless thronging spheres of light and shadow, of sweets
    and pain,
In this universe, resplendent from its germ atomic springing,
  Growing, varying, forthshooting world on world as flower on
    flower,
There is room for all we dream of ever in Fancy's wildest winging
  Save the Spirit's immortal heritage and a Father of love and
    power ?——
Suddenly o'er the trees without the muffled shore-like music
    streaming
  Broke upon my languid senses with its deep melodious psalm,
And I rose and loosed the shutter, and the moon in heaven was
    beaming,
  And I flung my cloak about me, wandering out in the woods of
    balm.

III.

Now, as the winds around me warble, as the earth on its orbit
    wheeleth,
  And I seem in the stir and music drifting far in the deeps of air,

All the subtle and gorgeous beauty that the fleshly veil concealeth
Openeth in my sight, revealing miracle after miracle bare;
Thick as dust in the desert hurricane whirl the worlds in their
    mystic dances,
Narrowing, widening, in their circles, round and round in
    wildering flight;
Shoot the comets from the abysses, meteors hurl their myriad
    lances,
In the mystery of motion, in the mystery of light;
Miracle of the orbs unnumbered, miracle of the life unfailing,—
Man and beast and bird and worm and herb and fruit and
    waving tree,—
Sweeps before me, sways me, thrills me, through the shoreless ether
    sailing,
Draws my heart to an unseen Presence in a rare exultancy. . . .

—*From " Stories of Wicklcw."*

ONE IN THE INFINITE.

I.

ROLL on, and, with thy rolling crust
    That round thy poles thou twirlest,
Roll with thee, Earth, this grain of dust,
    As through the Vast thou whirlest;
On, on through zones of dark and light
    Still waft me, blind and reeling,
Around the sun, and with *his* flight
    In wilder orbits wheeling.

II.

Speed on through deeps without a shore,
    This Atom with thee bearing,
Thyself a grain of dust—no more—
    'Mid fume of systems flaring.

Ah, what am I to thirst for power,
　　Or pore on Nature's pages,—
Whirled onward, living for an hour,
　　And dead through endless ages ?
　　　　　　—*From " One in the Infinite."*

CLOUD-SHADOWS.

I.

CLOUD-SHADOWS fly over the valley—
　　Shadow and gleam, shadow and gleam ;
No gleam in the heart without shadow—
　　Shadow and gleam ;
And the sun-glimmer lies in the grasses,
　　And brightens the kingscup's gold,
And shivers away, to vanish
　　In gloom and cold.

II.

Sun-glimmers fly over the ocean—
　　Glimmer and shade, glimmer and shade ;
No shade in the heart without glimmer—
　　Glimmer and shade ;
And the cloud-shadow lies on the ripples,
　　And darkens the seabird's white,
And quivers away, to vanish
　　In warmth and light.
　　　　　　—*From " One in the Infinite."*

THE OLD LIFE AND THE NEW.

I.

O PAST, old Past, fair life and sweet long-ended,
　　Why backward wilt thou draw my face, and twine
My love with that from which my feet have wended,
．　And whence I would go forward nor repine ?

II.

Drear are the moors, and yonder, high up-heaping
    Their brown bleak heads, the mountains fold my way,
Yet still in sunlight is that sweet Plain sleeping,
    And thither feebly still my heart will stray.

III.

Farewell, alas, farewell, old life lived over!
    I face yon track lost in the looming sky.
Take me, dark heights, black mists that wheel and hover!
    I must tramp on, or here lie down and die.

—From " One in the Infinite."

T. D. Sulliban.

M R. T. D. SULLIVAN, M.P., is a native of County
Cork, and was born near the town of Bantry
in the year 1827. Like most writers richly
endowed with literary talent, he wrote verse from the
days of his boyhood. In 1857 he joined the staff of the
Nation newspaper, and for many years was one of its
chief contributors in prose and verse. Among his best
known songs may be mentioned " Deep in Canadian Woods
We've Met," " Murty Hynes," and " God Save Ireland."
Various collections of Mr. Sullivan's works have been
published, and have had an extensive circulation. His
first two volumes, " Poems " and " Green Leaves," after
running through several editions, are now out of print.
His third volume " Prison Poems" was published in
1887, immediately after his release from Tullamore jail,
where he underwent a term of two months' imprisonment
for publishing, in his newspaper, the proceedings of
suppressed branches of the Irish National League contrary
to an Act of Parliament of that year. This little volume
reflects the greatest credit on Mr. Sullivan as a man, as a
politician, and as a poet. Although, as is well known, he
said and believed he was morally right in giving publicity
to those meetings, there is not one word of bitterness, nor
any spirit of hatred or revenge traceable in a single poem
throughout the volume. A rich vein of humour runs
through many of them, and they are entirely free from
strain or elaborate effort.

In 1892 Mr. Sullivan's latest work was published. It was entitled "Blanaid : and Other Poems from the Gælic" (Easton & Son). This volume consists of old Irish tales rendered into English verse, and shows the author's command of choice language and great powers of easy flowing versification.

Mr. Sullivan's career as a public man and politician is well known. He first entered Parliament in 1880 as Member for Westmeath, afterwards represented the College Green Division of the City of Dublin, and at present represents the Western Division of the County Donegal. He was Lord Mayor of Dublin in 1886, and so popular was he during his year of office that he was elected a second year.

THE PURSUIT.

From " BLANAID."

Ere yet the sky was tinted with morning's ruddy glow,
The Red Branch Knights assembled to chase the robber foe.
In three great bands divided, they quickly issued forth,
One eastward and one westward, the other towards the north;
The southern course Cuchullin preferred himself to tread
As if some instinct told him the way the knave had sped.
With scarce one moment's waiting two steeds of nimble pace
Brought up his shining chariot to bear him from the place;
Its ashen frame, high polished, with gold was barred and bound,
On oak wheels, ringed with silver, it lightly touched the ground;
Sharp spikes and blades projecting were set on either side
To cut through clustering foemen a passage clear and wide,
Even as a stalwart reaper through fields of yellowing wheat
Bring down their bristling glories in swathes about his feet.
There sat, equipped and ready, his trusty charioteer,
Whose hand was strong and steady, whose eye was quick and clear,
The faithful Leagh, in many a trying hour proved true,
And good a knight as any in all the great Creabh Ruah.

A frock of yellow deerskin was belted round his waist,
A bright-hued cloak above it his manly shoulders graced.
He placed upon his forehead the badge of burnished gold
That marked the noble office it was his pride to hold,
With his left hand he fingered the reins, held straight and tight,
A slender switch of hazel he flourished in his right.
In stepped Cuchullin gently ; one urging-word from Leagh,
And quick his willing coursers went Munster-wards away.
Full many a league they travelled, close watching, day and night
For signs and marks to show them the robber's line of flight,
Till on the lands of Sulchoid, not far in front they spied
The gray man in his chariot with Blanaid by his side.   [pace,
"Now Leagh," exclaimed the chieftain, "put on your quickest
Let not the villain foil us and give us fresh disgrace ;
Whip up your steeds to fury ; on, faster, faster yet,
Till face to face confronted the clown and I have met.
Full well I know this combat my utmost skill will try,
But it shall be decisive for he or I must die.
Observe me in the battle ; if pleased with what you see,
Speak not a word of boasting, give out no shout for me ;
But if a slow, unskilful, and feeble fight I wage,
Then taunt me, and revile me, and sting me into rage ;
That so with added venom in every thrust and blow,
And all the strength of madness, I may assail my foe."
Leagh gave the wished-for promise, but soon the fight was o'er,
The gray man fought and conquered by magic art once more,
He laid the Ulster chieftain nigh lifeless on the ground,
To mock him and to shame him his hands and feet he bound,
And, still more cruel insult—the worst that could be known—
He clipped his flowing ringlets, he sheared them to the bone.
And taking as a trophy one silken shining braid,
His southward way resuming, went forward with Blanaid.

AT THE GATE.

From " PRISON POEMS."

OF all the letters sent to me
   To cheer my prison days,
To bring me love and sympathy,
   To buoy me up with praise,
'Tis only some that come to hand,
   For—lest they'd harm the State—
A lot are held, I understand,
   Impounded at " The Gate."

They will not be destroyed, I'm told,
   Whate'er their nature be,
But just as safe as hoarded gold
   They'll all be kept for me ;
Perhaps their interest may increase
   As they go out of date,
But on the day of my release
   I'll get them at " The Gate."

I'll have to pass—the time is near—
   Another portal through ;
Ah, would I had no cause to fear
   What there will meet my view !
A long account, a large amount
   Of errors small and great—
A woful tale to make me quail
   And tremble at " The Gate."

Yet let me hope that mixed with those
   Some brighter things may be,
And that the prayers that oft arose
   From loving hearts for me,
Were never lost, cast down, or crost,
   But went to heaven straight,
And, by God's will, are potent still
   To help me through " The Gate."

L' ENVOI.

BEAUTY, or Poet, Sage, or Wit adieu :
   Our task is done : these simple, homely lays
   Of life, and love, and prayer, and ordered praise ;
Tinged, now, with colour caught from sky of blue,
Anon, enshadowed with the gloom of yew
    In graveyard grown, but flecked, even then, with rays
    Of Hope's own sunshine prophesying days
Of good to come ; here end with wish for you,

That as in happy, fairy times of old
   The man, who, wand'ring round some lonely lis,
    Came sudden on a solitary sprite
And held him fast, found heaps of hoarded gold ;
   So may you chance on some true wealth through this
    Small fay of minstrel lore—good night. Good night.
                                  G. R. B.